# ALL IN THE SEASONING

## EDITED BY
## KATHERINE V. FORREST

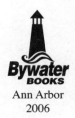

Bywater BOOKS

Ann Arbor
2006

# ALL IN THE SEASONING

# CONTENTS

# ALL IN THE SEASONING

## R. Gay

What Lillian remembered most about her childhood was the traditional soup her mother made every New Year's Eve. During the holiday season, the entire family gathered at her grandmother's house to celebrate. Her mother, grandmother, aunts and cousins would busy themselves in the kitchen while catching up on family news—Julianne pregnant again, Jean cheating on his wife—stories flying back and forth over cutting boards laden with fresh vegetables and pots steaming fragrantly. The men would sit in the living room, nursing rum and cokes, gossiping as only men can do. With the family spread from Haiti to Canada to the United States, the holidays were the only time when everyone came together to celebrate not only the New Year, but the ever-growing family as well.

The preparation of *la soupe traditionelle* was an all-day

process, and a tradition dating back to before the French had occupied Haiti. Lillian recalled the excitement she felt each New Year's Eve as she and her mother walked to the Korean market on the corner of the street they lived on. Lillian took seriously her duty of helping her mother and grandmother, solemnly inspecting the butternut squash, squeezing crisp green heads of cabbage, searching for the perfect onions and the tenderest cuts of beef. At these times, Lillian's mother would smile fondly at her daughter as she chattered, and slowly explored each aisle of the small market, imitating her mother's every move.

Lillian looked at her watch impatiently. She was in a hurry to get off work and catch the next train out of the city. Idly, she rearranged for the umpteenth time the five pencils and two pens splayed in a coffee mug on her desk. As the *Twelve Days of Christmas* began playing on the radio, Lillian winced. It wasn't that she hated the holidays, but she had sat around the office all day waiting for her vacation to start, and her patience was wearing thin. Around Lillian, her co-workers were in similar states of bored agitation, willing away the last hour of the workday. Lillian stretched out her long legs and glanced at the stack of files demanding her attention. Pulling her long braids into a ponytail, she briefly considered actually getting some work done but pushed the files to the side and out of her line of vision. Pointless, definitely pointless. Her caseload would have to wait until after the first of the year. I deserve a break today,

2

she rationalized. Sighing, she picked up the phone and started dialing.

Sabrina tossed a sweater into the open suitcase on the bed. The music of Bob Marley blared through the apartment and the bedroom was in shambles. At the last minute, her girlfriend Lillian had decided that she was indeed going to bring Sabrina home to meet her family. Every night for the past month, the two had debated back and forth about whether or not it was time for Sabrina to meet her in-laws. Sabrina had finally given up, deciding that bad television and a frozen dinner with her own family would be less troubling than continuing the argument with Lillian. But now, everything had changed. She was going to nearby Connecticut, where Lillian's parents now lived. In less than a day she had to do laundry, pack, and find someone to take care of Mephistopheles, their overweight tabby cat. Sabrina chewed her lower lip, blowing her auburn bangs out of her face. She was forgetting something. As she burrowed through a pile of clothes, she heard the phone ringing and ran to turn the stereo down.

"Hello," she answered breathlessly.

"It's me," the voice on the other end replied glumly.

Sabrina smiled.

"Are you ready yet?"

Sabrina kicked some clothes under the bed. "I'm just about to leave for the train station."

They were both silent for a moment. "Honey, are you okay?" Sabrina asked gently.

"I've never brought a lover home before."

"Parents love me and I'll be on my best behavior, just for you."

Lillian chewed on the end of her pencil, wrapping the phone cord around her fingers. "It's not about whether or not you're on your best behavior. You're a woman."

"You don't say."

"Love the sarcasm. But you don't know my mother."

"Your mother and I will be fine."

"I know my family. They are . . . Haitian," Lillian stammered.

"They will hardly notice I'm a woman. Tell them I can change the oil in my car," Sabrina quipped.

"You don't have car."

Sabrina rolled her eyes. "Your family has to meet me sooner or later. After three years, I'd say that now is as good a time as any."

"I suppose you're right."

"I know I'm right and I've got to go. Don't want to be late, now do I?"

"Right. See you soon," Lillian replied wryly.

Sabrina stared at the phone, shaking her head. Lillian could be such a pessimist. This whole thing was being blown out of proportion. Zipping up her suitcase, she took a final survey of the apartment and headed for the train station.

Staring out the grimy window of the train, Lillian clenched Sabrina's hand with sweaty fingers. She had put off introducing her lover to her family for so long that she was giving herself an ulcer worrying about it now. It wasn't that she was ashamed of who she was, or Sabrina. It was more an irrational fear of losing her family and the fear irked Lillian. It felt so clichéd. But she didn't want to choose between her family and her lover. It wasn't a choice she was capable of making. She sat still, her body taut with tension. As the tall buildings faded, Lillian closed her eyes, breathing slowly.

Upon returning from the market, purchases in tow, Lillian and her mother would join her grandmother and her aunts and cousins in preparing the meat and vegetables. Lillian's father would go down to the basement and bring up the enormous pot which they would use for their soup. After her mother washed away the thick layer of dust, Lillian would carefully dry it with a hand towel and stare at her reflection in the bottom of the cavernous pot. The kitchen would grow unbearably hot and crowded but each woman had to have a hand in the creation of *la soupe traditionelle*. A blend of Creole and English filtered through the air and as Lillian sliced carrots, she would strain to understand what the adults were saying. Their conversations fascinated her and she anxiously looked forward to the day when she too could take part in those conversations.

Lillian's chest tightened as the train pulled into the tiny Connecticut rail station and she saw her mother standing alone on the platform. She liked to think of her parents as ageless creatures but now she was realizing that such was not the case. She couldn't help but notice that her mother was getting not only older but smaller. Astrid was a tiny woman, standing no taller than five feet. Her long black hair, streaked with silver, cascaded down her back. When people stopped to look at her they couldn't quite place her ancestry; her skin was light enough that she could hail from just about anywhere. Standing alone on the platform, she looked supremely confident and unaffected.

The train crawled to a halt and Lillian felt her heart stop. The squeaking brakes sounded unbearably loud. Suddenly, she could breathe again, her heart fluttering as she stood up. Sabrina tugged at the sleeve of Lillian's coat and reluctantly, Lillian grabbed her suitcase and went to meet her mother.

"Welcome to the beginning of the end," Lillian muttered under her breath.

Sabrina smiled brightly as they reached Lillian's mother. Lillian stiffly leaned over to kiss her mother on each cheek and just as stiffly introduced Sabrina. Wordlessly, the three headed for the car, Sabrina quietly observing the tense body language between Lillian and her mother. She took slight offense that Lillian's mother hadn't even bothered to greet her with more than a curt nod, but decided it was nothing. When they finally reached their destination, Sabrina jumped out of the car and sighed as her feet landed on the gravel drive, weary from a long day and the train ride up from New York City.

Lillian's family lived in a spacious home with a cold colonial exterior that belied the Caribbean atmosphere inside. Her two younger brothers, Alain and Carl, burst through the front door rushing to greet their sister. Sabrina watched timidly from the side as a throng of relatives converged upon them. Hugs and laughter of greeting filled the Creole-spiced air.

Sabrina smiled wistfully as her thoughts wandered to her own family. They weren't especially close, but they were the only family she had. For some reason, spending the holidays with Lillian's family made her wistful for her mom and dad and their quirky traditions. She was completely out of place and feeling like a minority for the first time in her life. Lillian's family was so different and they clearly hadn't taken notice of this American standing on the fringe.

When Lillian finally broke free from the familial grasp, she grabbed Sabrina's hand, pulling her into the mix.

"Everyone," Lillian interrupted, switching from the Creole they were speaking to English. "I want you to meet Sabrina, my . . . my . . ." she faltered, "roommate."

Sabrina arched an eyebrow and rocked back and forth on her heels.

Lillian wrinkled her nose, sliding her arm around Sabrina's shoulders. "Actually, she's my girlfriend. She is my roommate too, but . . ."

Lillian exhaled slowly, waiting for the silence to erupt into sound. Her family nodded politely, some in confusion, others offering weak handshakes. Lillian's mother stared at the couple coldly, and headed into the house. Quickly, the others followed Astrid. Lillian and Sabrina stood on the porch, breathing the cold evening air. The shutter-framed windows stared emptily at the couple.

Lillian rubbed her forehead. "Merry Christmas to us."

She had always been attracted to women. At the all-girl Catholic school she attended for twelve years, while her classmates went on about the boys Lillian was thinking about holding hands and taking naps with the girls. Each year when her family got together, asking where her boyfriend was, Lillian would shrug off their questions, or invent a Mr. Wonderful of the Month. As Lillian grew older and was finally able to share in the gossip while the women made soup, she felt herself growing apart from her family. There was plenty she could share but nothing her family would want to hear.

She and Sabrina had met years ago at a writer's conference. It wasn't love at first sight, but over time they had fallen in love and Lillian had longed to tell her mother how happy she and Sabrina were. Her brother Alain shared such conversations with their parents, Lillian thought bitterly. He was married to a woman, but heaven forbid she did the same.

On the morning of New Year's Eve, Lillian and Sabrina sat at the table in the breakfast nook sipping from mugs of hot coffee. They had been in Connecticut for a week; a very long week. Sabrina was sore from sleeping on a couch that was too narrow and too short. It had gone unsaid that she and Lillian were forbidden to share a bed. When they had made preparations for bed that first night, a set of sheets and a thin pillow lay waiting on the couch in the family room for Sabrina, while one of the guest rooms had been made up for Lillian. The couple received the cold shoulder from most of the family. No one was rude exactly, but they were deliberately left out of conversations and family outings, as if they were somehow invisible in the mix. Both women were more than ready to return to their lives in New York City. Lillian's thin face was drawn, shadows darkening her eyes.

"I'm so sorry I brought you into this," Lillian whispered.

Sabrina reached across the table and covered Lillian's hand with hers. "It's not that bad."

"You're a terrible liar."

"Your parents might have made me sleep on the floor."

Lillian ran her hands through her braids and scowled. "I am twenty-seven. I have a degree. I have a career. I should be allowed to make my own choices when it comes to my love life."

"That would be too easy. Besides, it wouldn't be a family holiday without a healthy dose of melodrama."

Lillian smirked. "I wish I could be as noble as you."

"Sweetheart, it's not nobility. It's understanding. You know how strange my parents can be. One week they adore us and send us cruise pamphlets. Two weeks later, my mom is trying to straighten me out. Nobody's perfect."

"You are full of wisdom, aren't you?"

"It is indeed hard being a genius."

"The good news is that we're out of here on the first train tomorrow morning, and hopefully we can forget about this little family experiment of mine. I'm almost looking forward to returning to work." Lillian slid away from the table. "I'm going on the porch for a cigarette. I'll be back."

"Don't your parents hate when you smoke?"

"Do I care?" Lillian said with a laugh, blowing Sabrina a kiss.

Shivering, she wrapped her bathrobe tightly around her body and sat on the old porch swing. She could see her breath in the morning air. Pulling a crumpled pack of cigarettes from a pocket, she folded her legs under her. In the distance the sun was rising and the stillness around her was comforting. Sighing, she slid a cigarette between her lips and exhaled a long stream of smoke. She loved her family, really she did. They were loving and tightly knit. Even spread apart they managed to remain close with a constant stream of phone calls and letters. When something went wrong, she knew she could call any one of her aunts or uncles for help and advice. But when it came to her relationship with Sabrina, the generosity had disappeared. She never expected them to be thrilled that she was gay, but a little understanding would be nice.

When she had come out to her mother, there were none of the histrionics you read about in those self-help books. Astrid had simply nodded stiffly and pretended that she hadn't heard. Lillian had felt a twinge of disappointment at the apparent lack of response and now that twinge had festered into bitterness. Anger and tears would have been far better than the cold silence she had dealt with for the past several years. As she remembered the warm hug her spawn-producing sister-in-law had received from Astrid, Lillian felt a surge of jealousy.

And Sabrina. Although they were miserable, Lillian was glad her lover was here with her. Her presence made this entire ordeal bearable. She smiled as she recalled the warmth of Sabrina's hand over hers at the breakfast table. They had their disagreements but they shared a good—no, a great relationship. Lillian enjoyed having someone to come home to after a long day at work and she enjoyed waking up to see Sabrina smiling down at her. On Saturdays they went to the Farmer's Market together and Sundays were spent lazing in their apartment or wandering around the city. Last week, Sabrina had lost her temper because Lillian hadn't done the laundry in over two weeks. Lillian had acted as chastely as possible, but Sabrina's eyes twitched in the most adorable way when she was mad, and soon they were throwing dirty clothes at each other and had fallen to the floor laughing.

Lillian tapped the ashes from her cigarette into a nearby plant and began rocking slowly. In one more day she and Sabrina would be on a train leaving all this behind, and she knew she wouldn't be returning for a good long time. Standing up, Lillian flicked the remainder of her cigarette into the carpet of snow and watched as the flame extinguished.

Taking a deep breath, she stepped back into the warmth of the house, feeling remarkably cold. The rest of the household had awakened and Lillian found her parents standing in the kitchen. Her dad nodded in her direction as he brewed a fresh pot of coffee. Her mother was absorbed in washing the large pot for *la soupe traditionelle*.

"Good morning," Lillian said, sliding out of her robe.

She shivered, rubbing her bare arms. Her T-shirt and boxers provided little relief from the morning chill. Two empty coffee cups sat at the kitchen table, but Sabrina was nowhere in sight.

"You could at least acknowledge my presence, Mother," Lillian continued, her voice laced with irritation.

Lillian's mother stopped, resting her hands on the counter. "You should have known better than to bring that girl home," Astrid spat in her heavily accented voice.

"You knew I was bringing Sabrina home, S-a-b-r-i-n-a. She has a name." Lillian clenched her jaw, her breathing measured.

She could see the veins on her mother's hands bulging as her fingers clenched into tight fists. "You can do what you choose where you live, but how dare you throw it in my face."

Lillian just stared. Her father quietly disappeared, leaving his wife and daughter alone. Lillian said, "I don't want to argue about this anymore."

"I'm not arguing. I am telling you I do not want this in my house."

"This? I can't even touch my lover without looking over my shoulder and you are acting like we're fucking on the kitchen table."

Lillian's mother slammed the pot into the sink and turned.

The pot slowly clattered still and mother and daughter looked at each other, their dark eyes flashing.

"I can't believe you," Lillian stuttered, running out of the kitchen.

Once in the safety of her bedroom, she leaned against the door, dropping to the floor. Tears burned down her face. Sabrina, who had been lying on the bed reading a book, quickly crossed the room and knelt next to her lover.

"What's wrong?" Sabrina asked hoarsely.

"I just want to go home," Lillian mumbled into Sabrina's sweatshirt.

Sabrina bit her lower lip and stroked Lillian's hair away from her face. Tenderly, she ran a finger under Lillian's chin, lifting her face. With butterfly kisses, she wiped the tears away and brushed her lips across Lillian's.

"They do love you, though they have a strange way of showing it."

"How could I tell?" Lillian asked, almost chuckling.

"You just have to look very closely, like reading between the lines. You know what this is all about . . . mourning the person they wanted you to be before they can accept the person you are, blah blah blah, so on and so forth. It could be much worse, and you know it."

"Is that my spoon full of sugar, Miss Mary Poppins?"

Sabrina pulled Lillian to her feet and led her to the bed, wrapping her arms around her lover as they lay down. "Something like that. Besides which . . . it's New Year's Eve. I'm thinking lots of champagne while no one's looking. I get to taste this great soup you're always babbling about, and I actually like your brothers, who are the only people who have bothered to speak to me since we got here."

Lillian managed a small smile. "Yeah, they are okay in moderate doses. I hated them when we were kids."

"It was your job to hate them just like it's your job to be overly sensitive when it comes to dealing with your mother."

"I suppose you're right." Lillian looked over at the door. "Did you lock it?"

Sabrina waggled her tongue and winked. "Of course I did."

Lillian pretended to blush, fanning herself with her hands. "Why, whatever for?"

"The better to seduce you with, of course."

Lillian wiped her face on her sleeve and rolled onto her back. "Ah, but of course."

As Lillian sniffled loudly, Sabrina laughed. "Now that . . . that is sexy."

Lillian shrugged. "I do what I can."

"Show me what you can do," Sabrina whispered softly.


At the stroke of midnight, the entire family would gather in the dining room to say a prayer. It was more than a prayer. It was a time to give thanks for the past. It was a time of looking forward to the New Year. Starting with her grandmother and ending with the youngest, they went around the room speaking to God, and to each other. Lillian would wait nervously for her time to come, always unsure until that final moment just what she was going to say. She always felt everything had been said by the time her turn came around and she much preferred to taste the soup, which had a different flavor each year, than listen to the adults going on and on. As she matured, she grew to appreciate just how important this time of sharing was.

Lillian heard the clock chime midnight and felt her stomach clench. Sabrina was pacing the length of the small bedroom, muttering under her breath.

"We should be heading downstairs," said Lillian, quietly.

"We should be heading out of town."

"What happened to your good mood?"

"I packed it."

"It's almost over, I swear. Please, let's just get this over with."

Sabrina smirked. "We could always strip naked and greet them in our birthday suits. Wouldn't that be a sight to see?"

"That's a mighty tempting proposition."

Sabrina hugged Lillian from behind and inhaled the clean scent of Lillian's hair. Nibbling her lover's ear, Sabrina said, "It would be the highlight of this trip. Your family needs a little shaking up."

Lillian shook her head laughing as she reluctantly extracted herself from Sabrina's embrace. "I couldn't agree with you more, but now is not the time."

"You can be so square sometimes."

"And it's one of the many reasons you adore me."

"Keep telling yourself that."

"I will," Lillian answered solemnly, pulling Sabrina down-stairs.

The pot of soup sat in the middle of the table, steaming fragrantly. Lillian allowed herself a small smile as she remembered the many years she had spent gathered around this table. Her father quickly poured champagne into the empty glasses, with cider for the children who were hoping for just one taste of the forbidden drink. When everyone finally quieted down, Lillian's grandmother stood up and began the prayer. When Astrid stood for her turn, Lillian's fingers gripped the stem of her glass.

"As I stand here with my family, which grows every year, I can almost say that I am happy. There are four generations in this room tonight." Lillian's nephew giggled from under the table where he hid. "The one thing preventing my complete happiness is how my only daughter chooses to live her life. I can only ask God to show her the correct path."

Lillian cleared her throat and felt everyone staring at her. When it came to her turn, the familiar dread did not wash over her. Lillian knew exactly what she wanted to say.

Lillian looked directly at her mother. "I love all of you, unconditionally. I love everyone that I love, unconditionally. While blood may be thicker than water, this woman," Lillian said, gesturing to Sabrina, "has loved me unconditionally for the past three years. That's more than most of you around this table can say. We will stand around this table again only when you all can love and accept us unconditionally. You can disapprove but you have to respect me. You have to respect us. That's my hope for the New Year."

Lillian leaned into Sabrina, so close that their lips were almost touching. She paused, feeling Sabrina's breath falling against her neck.

The rest of the family eyed the couple warily. Astrid paled. Sabrina's heart pounded under the stares of those around her. Lillian inched closer, tentatively brushing her lips across Sabrina's. She pulled Sabrina's hand into hers and parting her lips she kissed her lover passionately. As they pulled apart Sabrina stared at Lillian with admiration and a hint of surprise.

Lillian caught her brother's eye and he grinned, giving her a small thumbs up. Astrid's cheeks twitched but she stood silently. The rest of the family was clearly uncomfortable, shifting nervously from side to side, looking anywhere but at each other. Grace dictated their silence but Lillian could imagine what they were thinking. One of Lillian's cousins stood up and gave a halting speech about a Happy New Year or some such. The tense moment passed. Tradition continued.

Each year, when everyone had had their fill of *la soupe traditionelle*, the women would send a bit of the remainder home with each family. The bone from the meat was boiled into a stock that would store until the next year. Each year, this stock was put into the new soup, adding a certain richness. When these details were taken care of, the family sat around the fireplace sharing old stories and creating new ones. The young were taught the history of the family from the sugar cane fields of Haiti to Ellis Island thirty years ago to where they were now. Her grandmother would sit in a comfortable chair, frail hands holding an illicit cup of rum and coffee. Her eyes would close, and a story would begin. She would speak of her childhood, walking barefoot to school each day, how she curled her toes around the warm dust. She talked about the time when Astrid was a child, playing with baby chicks in the yard. How an enraged mother hen chased after Astrid, pecking at her little hands. How, to protect her daughter, Lillian's grandmother had grabbed an ax and chopped the mother hen's head off. Hundreds of miles away from home, an ancestral fabric was woven, preserving the strength of the family.

Upon returning to New York, Lillian and Sabrina quickly fell into the comfortable pattern of their lives. As a child advocate for the District Attorney's office, Lillian had more cases than she could handle. Children were neglected no matter the season, and the stress of dealing with her clients was a welcome relief from thinking about her vacation. Sabrina worried as she watched her partner shutting herself off, but didn't know how to help. She didn't want Lillian to lose her family and she didn't want to lose Lillian. The situation felt hopeless, and she could only watch, and wait, and worry more.

Lillian stared wistfully at the clock. She was working this New

Year's Eve. She and Sabrina had decided that staying in their loft was slightly more appealing than dealing with either of their families. The same shuffle of Christmas music crackled from the radio, and she had already rearranged her desk seven times. Forty-five minutes to go. Lillian and her mother had barely spoken over the past year. In fact, only her brothers and sometimes her father kept in touch. Lillian drained the last of the stale coffee from a Styrofoam cup, carelessly tossing it into the trash. The office was disturbingly silent. The rest of the staff were away, enjoying their holidays and Lillian felt like throwing herself a pity party. Twenty-seven minutes to go. Lillian pictured Sabrina at home, sliding across the hardwood floors in her thick wool socks. Suddenly, she wanted to be there and nowhere else.

Gathering her briefcase and coat, she left the office and walked the few blocks to the subway, ignoring the revelers milling around her.

Wearily, Lillian climbed the stairs out of the subway station and headed for the loft. As she passed the market on the corner, she paused, eyeing the fresh produce. She remembered trailing after her mother as they shopped for *la soupe traditionelle*, and how important it was to find the perfect ingredients. She remembered the tiny beads of sweat that fell into the soup as she stood next to her mother at the stove, slowly stirring the thick broth. She remembered everything she had ever known about where she came from. She entered the market, sighing softly as warm air and strange smells swirled around her. For a brief moment she felt lost, but quickly riffled through her brief-case and muttered, "Yes," as she found a greasy recipe card lodged between the pages of her date book.

*La Soupe Traditionelle*

*Two heads of cabbage*
*Peas*
*Butternut Squash*
*Leeks*
*Potatoes*
*Turnips*
*Carrots*
*Onions*
*Cilantro and Parsley*
*Beef Tenderloin*
*—Cook meat until tender over low heat. Season to taste with garlic, salt, black pepper and hot peppers.*
*—Add water and previous year's stock.*
*—Add vegetables according to required cooking time for desired consistency.*

# A Hot Christmas Lunch

## Cynthia Price

I stood next to the Christmas tree, its stick-like branches hanging heavy with fake cotton-wool dollops of snow, and stared through the frost-haloed window panes at the flowering bougainvillea at the bottom of the garden. On the front lawn, framed by the rampant display of Christmas-red blossoms, I could see Josie's nephews bounding bare-chested through the sprinkler's rainbow-tinted spray, screaming in joyous pain each time the cold water touched their hot bodies. At the edge of the picture, just out of the sprinkler's reach, the boys' fathers lay limply in garden chairs, nursing beer glasses against their hairy paunches as they supervised their sons' activities.

Although the French doors had been propped wide open, the sitting room sweated like a sauna from the steam drifting through from the kitchen, adding to the already unbearable humidity of another hot Christmas Day in Kwa Zulu Natal in the Republic of South Africa. I was almost tempted to strip down and join the boys under their shower, imagining the cool sting of the water as it rinsed the sticky sweat from my body, but decided against it. I was already under a strained welcome and had better restrain myself.

Spurts of loudly whispered words darted out from the direction of the kitchen above the sounds of clattering pots and pans as roast potatoes were turned over, sauces stirred and the stuffed turkey poked at just one more time. Every time the oven door was pulled open or another pot of vegetables was drained off over the sink, a fresh cloud of steam vented into the rest of the house.

My Josie's voice was coming through the loudest, trying to deafen out the protests of her sister, Brittany, whose house I was invading on this traditionally family-only occasion. Elise, being only the wife of the brother and knowing her place in the scheme of things, voiced her opinion only when asked for it, her high-pitched giggle agreeing with Brittany's emphatic statements.

"How's your beer doing?"

I turned to see Charles standing in the doorway, waving an empty, froth-encrusted glass at the almost full glass in my hand.

"Still fine, thanks!" I raised my beer in his direction and felt a dribble of condensation trickle down my wrist before it dropped onto the carpet.

He stood for a moment and listened to the debating voices rising and falling over the cooking frenzy. The golden flecks in his eyes faded, leaving only dark stormy pupils, reminding me of Josie's eyes when she gets really mad. He spun on his heel and headed toward the kitchen, punching the swing-doors open with his free fist.

I heard the deep murmur of his voice but couldn't hear his words. By the time he came back out again, smiling at his newly refilled glass of beer, the women's voices had been silenced. The only sounds coming from the kitchen were the clanging of pots and the high-pitched squeal of the oven door opening for yet another turkey check.

I watched Charles as he made his way back outside, taking large strides across the sitting room carpet while wiping his cool glass over his bare chest. He stood with legs apart on the stone paving of the veranda and shouted for the children to dry off and get ready for lunch, before striding across the lawn to resume his garden seat next to Gerrit.

The boys stampeded through the doorway and I huddled myself closer to the snowbound Christmas tree, defending my beer from possible spillage over the aesthetically wrapped and beribboned empty boxes lying under the spreading boughs. My arm brushed against a hanged snowman who threatened to fall off his perch and become impaled on a pointy plastic snowflake tied onto a lower branch. I reached out and steadied the snowman as four pairs of bare feet thumped past me and bounced across the carpet. Towel-tousled heads bumped up and down as the boys danced around the table shouting their admiration at the decorations. Fingers pointed at the crackers on the side plates, the candles standing to attention in the middle of the table just waiting to be lit and the bunches of plastic holly and bright red berries artistically scattered across the table cloth.

I smelled Josie standing behind me before her hand touched my shoulder. "You okay?" I heard her saying and I breathed in deeply to inhale the comforting smell of her perfume.

I shrugged as I turned around to face her. "I've had better days!" I smiled at her. The golden flecks in her eyes dimmed, so I smiled harder and raised a fingertip to gently brush the damp patch of skin under her lower lip. Josie smiled back at me and, for a brief moment, the golden sparkle returned to her eyes.

Brittany's voice screeched through the air from the kitchen doorway: "Please! Not in front of the children!"

The children stopped their dancing around the table to watch me wiping the sweat off their aunty's chin, decided the action was not as interesting as their mother's tone of voice had made it out to be and continued with their noisy war-dance.

Brittany continued to stand in the doorway, hands on hips, mouth tightened up into a shrivelled holly berry. Elise's head bobbed up and down over Brittany's shoulder trying to catch a glimpse of whatever orgiastic ritual we were performing in front of the children. I tightened my own lips to prevent the grin which threatened to break through, and slowly removed my finger from Josie's face.

Brittany's attention switched to the horde of children

24

swarming around the lunch table. "If you boys don't get dressed now, there will be no lunch for you. Move it!"

The children broke their circling pattern and thudded in a single file down the passageway, their voices muted into loud whispers. I saw Brittany's eyes searching the room for her next target and kept both of my hands firmly around my beer glass.

The damp patch on the back of my blouse caught a sudden twist of breeze and I turned around to see Charles and Gerrit standing in the doorway like twins, beer glasses held against hairy chests as though they were singing the national anthem at a rugby match, knobbly knees sticking out under long baggy shorts, eyes wide open and questioning, but mouths wisely kept closed.

Brittany had found her next target. "And if you two men think you are sitting down to lunch dressed like that, you have another think coming!" she squalled at them, her bright red lipstick catching a glint of sunshine. "I am trying to have a proper meal here. You have ten minutes to make yourselves presentable!"

She twisted around on her heel and almost bumped into Elise who was still bobbing up and down trying to catch a glimpse of the action in the sitting room. After a few sidestepping movements with her sister-in-law under the mistletoe which hung in the galley doorway, Brittany took her tight berry lips haughtily back into the kitchen.

By the time the turkey and trimmings were laid out on the table, the menfolk and boyfolk had returned, suitably attired in shirts and ties, ready to spend the meal tugging in irritation at their collars.

The lunch had been perfectly prepared, but my stomach was not ready for it. Each mouthful had to be forced down my throat as I wriggled uncomfortably against my damp chair-back. I had to wipe my forehead continuously to prevent the drips of sweat from collecting on my eyebrows and threatening to oversalt my food. By the time the steamed pudding was carried through with its blue-burning surface, I was already too bloated to consume another morsel of food.

Apart from the squirming of the boys and the constant collar-tugging of the men, the lunch party had behaved to Brittany's satisfaction. Of course, I had been placed at the furthest distance away from Josie to remove any possible temptation to embarrass my fellow diners by caressing her at the table or tickling her legs with my toes or leaning forward to kiss her on the lips above the damp patch of skin I had so rudely fondled earlier in the day. Apart from the profuse sweating, I behaved like a regular lady.

Brittany stood up and gave us all a bright berry smile before leaning forward to gather the empty pudding plates. "Why don't you guys go down to the beach to cool off a bit while Elise and I tidy up?" she suggested.

I stretched backwards in my chair, rubbed my swollen stomach and offered her a peace-offering of a smile. "That really was good, Brittany. Thanks. But it's only fair that Josie and I help with the dishes."

She waved a hand. "No really!" she insisted. "Elise and I can manage. You go on down to the beach with the boys."

The men and boys were excused from the table to change back into swimming costumes while the women carted the empty plates back to the steam-filled kitchen. I scraped leftovers into the bin and stacked the plates alongside the pot-cluttered sink. A fresh outbreak of sweat spread across my back and along my bra-strap and I wiped my forehead with my wrist to prevent the salty drops from stinging my eyes. As I scraped another pile of plates I forced myself not to comment on how more comfortable it would have been to eat cold meats and salads on paper plates in the shade of the Mkuhla tree out in the garden.

As I stacked the last plate, the boys came skipping down the passageway, flicking each other with their beach towels and shouting their readiness to head down to the beach.

"Are you sure we can't help with the dishes?" I asked Brittany again.

"Sure!" she said, shooing us from the kitchen with both her hands. "Get out of here!"

Charles and Gerrit walked the two blocks downhill to Uvongo Beach with the boys skipping around their feet, while Josie and I followed in the car. My stomach was so full I could not trust my legs to carry the extra weight down the steep hill. If I fell over I wouldn't stop rolling until I reached the beach and I had visions of floating out over the Indian Ocean and beaching somewhere in Australia.

A slight breeze had come up from the North, flittering over

the salty moisture which had built up on my skin and helping to cool me down. I lay back in the sand, keeping a diplomatically discreet distance between myself and Josie so that Gerrit would have nothing untoward to report back to his wife about our behavior. The boys hopped around at the edge of the water, splashing each other and squealing as boys do when playing in water. Every time they moved further into the breakers they would be shouted back by their respective fathers with words of caution about having just eaten a large meal and "You don't want to drown, do you?"

I closed my eyes and felt the sun burn red blotches against my eyelids. My toes dug through the hot upper layer of sand, looking for the cooler patches just beneath the surface. A smile played inside me as the tightness of my stomach began to ease. I listened to the happy screams of the boys as they rolled around in the water where it rushed back and forth up the beach.

My ears detected that one of the screams had changed from happiness to pain and I sat up hurriedly. Brittany and Gerrit's younger son was holding onto his arm and running up the beach towards us, screaming, his toes tripping in the loose sand.

"Bluebottles!" I shouted, as I jumped up, "Better call the other boys out of the water now!"

Gerrit and Charles just sat looking at each other.

Josie crawled along the sand to grab hold of the crying child and clutched him close to her chest to soothe him. She leaned over his head and called out to the other boys to get out of the water and watched as they grudgingly dragged their feet along the sand.

I scrabbled across the hot dunes to the scrub growing along the back edge of the beach, my eyes searching over the scant greenery for the familiar fat leaves and bright pink anemone-like flowers of the vygies that grow all along the coastline. I dropped to my knees and broke off a handful of fat leaves to take back to the patient.

The boy's crying slowed to a whimper as I squeezed the juice from the leaves onto the red scalding on his forearm. He turned around to look at the sticky gum coating the red welt and then offered me a brave smile.

"Better?" I asked.

He nodded and a stray tear dropped off his eyelashes to join the droplets of sea water on his face.

"I think you've had enough beach for one day! Do you want us to take you home?"

He nodded again and raised his uninjured arm to dry his face.

Josie wrapped the boy up in his towel and carried him to the car. She hopped from one foot to the other on the scalding tarmac while I opened up the doors and let the breeze cool down the oven-like interior. I watched as she swayed from side to side, trying not to lose her balance with the heavy weight cradled in her arms.

When the car had cooled down sufficiently to not roast the boy like a turkey, Josie laid him down on the back seat and stood up to stretch her back muscles, while still tap-dancing on the tarred road. "I think we've had enough beach for one day too. Let's just drop him off with his mother and head off home."

"Couldn't agree more," I said, climbing into the passenger seat and waving the hot air around with my hands. "I think I've had more than enough Christmas fun for one day."

While Josie carried her nephew into the house, I sat in the car hoping that her family goodbyes would not take too long. The backs of my legs were sticking to the car seat and a new river had sprung a leak down my back.

I didn't have long to wait. Josie came sprinting down the pathway, hopscotched around the car and threw herself into the driver's seat. She sat and stared at the road ahead, letting her fingertips dance across the hot steering wheel. A naughty smile danced a matching step across her whole face.

"What?" I asked.

"The dishes haven't even been touched!" she said, shaking her head in mock disapproval and making a berry mouth to match her sister's.

"So? It's so bloody hot, they deserve to take a break from all the cooking before doing the dishes."

She turned and grinned at me. "You know that bright red lipstick that Brittany always insists on wearing at Christmas?"

"Her Christmas lipstick? Yeah! What about it?" I wriggled in my seat to try and unstick my legs from the synthetic upholstery.

"Elise was wearing it!" she offered me with a taunting grin.

"Okay! So Elise was wearing Brittany's lipstick. What's so weird about that—apart from the fact that your sister and sister-in-law share the same bad taste in make-up?"

Josie at last strapped on her seat-belt and turned the key in the ignition. She turned once more to face me. "On her neck, my sweetie? On her neck!"

# THE ILLEGALS

# Kathy Porter

Behind the wheel, driving around the desert, I would not think about thirsty Mexicans. I would think, simply, about turkey and cranberries. The truck bumped solidly on the dirt road. It was a new truck, maintained by a crew of persnickety mechanics, the kind of men who have low tolerance for loose bolts or dust under the hood. Its wheels were firm under me, heavy-duty government shock absorbers a cushion against the washboard. I'd just responded to a call on the shortwave from a rancher who said he'd spotted a group of illegals walking along a wash on his property. By the time I got to his place they'd disappeared into the brush, leaving behind a candy wrapper and an empty plastic water jug.

A desert tortoise crawled across the road. There's a woman in these parts who has spent the last twenty years marking each tortoise she finds with a big red number on its underbelly. I got out of the truck and picked up the guy crawling his way across the dirt. Number one hundred eighty-nine. I put him down on the opposite side of the road and took off my windbreaker. The sun warmed the back of my neck. The night before, Channel Four News had run another of those stories Arizonans can't get enough of: harsh winter weather back east, images of cars stuck in Michigan snow banks and harried commuters ankle-deep in slush. On the horizon the surveillance balloon drifted, a miniature white zeppelin in the flawless blue sky over the Huachuca Mountains. I would not think about my paycheck, about desperate Mexicans, the maddeningly slow construction of our house, or the calm view of the valley we can see now only from lawn chairs set on bare dirt. I would think about an unusually warm Thanksgiving, Fran's stuffing, her pumpkin pie, and a glass of good red wine.

The shortwave in the truck beeped. It was Fran, calling to ask me to stop at the Safeway for butter, a pineapple and fresh parsley. She cooks like crazy on holidays. She doesn't mind that it's just the two of us; we've gotten used to keeping to ourselves. It's best not to let too many people into our lives. No one around here wants to know a dyke teaches their first graders.

When I got home to our trailer she was in the kitchen mixing a bowl of cranberries. An extra pan of stuffing was on the stove.

"Smells like Thanksgiving in here," I said.

"Don't get ahead of yourself," she said. "And whoa, girl! Keep your fingers out of my stuffing." She swatted the air but I snatched a few crumbs anyway. I stepped close behind her, put the pinch of stuffing in her mouth and another in my own. I tasted sage, celery, and a hint of sausage.

"Got your groceries," I said. "I had to buy canned pineapple. There wasn't any fresh."

Fran frowned at the can. "I thought we'd eat in the new house tonight," she said. "Maybe bring in the space heater—just in case it gets a little chilly later on?"

I went to the shed to find the heater and the folding card table, then carried them to the new house and set them up on the cement floor in the middle of the living room. We'd get to watch the sunset through the plate glass window the two of us had installed last week. It was still dusty and full of our fingerprints. I went to get the Windex, and when I came back to clean the window, that's when I saw the woman emerge from behind the bush.

The late afternoon sun was in my eyes, so at first I thought the movement outside the house was a bird or a rabbit. I kept wiping, trying to capture the streaks, when I caught the movement again. Behind a creosote bush, fifty feet from the window, there was the woman. A Mexican woman. God almighty, not today. Fran would be calling from the trailer any minute to tell me the turkey was out of the oven. The woman had a baby in a cloth sling over her shoulder. And there behind her, holy crap, was a child, no more than four years old, wearing a red Pokemón T-shirt and

34

clutching her leg. A stained sweatshirt was tied around his waist.

The woman stepped out from behind the bush. Clumps of hair escaped her ponytail. She took the child's hand and they walked straight up to the window. She was lit from behind, and I held the damp paper towels up to block the sun.

"Momentito," I said through the window, my palm out. I walked through the front door to the outside of the house.

"De donde está?" I asked the woman. Where are you from? Her lips were dry and cracked from the sun, and she had a nose that belonged on the face of an Aztec goddess. She wore hiking boots that looked too large for her feet.

"Chiapas," she said. So she wasn't a regular crosser. Too far from home, and the children were too young.

"Adonde vaya?" I asked her. Where are you going?

"El Paso."

God. They'd been dumped by her smuggler, a coyote.

"Do you know where you are?" Before I moved from Boston I never suspected I'd need to learn a foreign language just to do my job. Last time I spoke to my father he called it a necessary evil. "A good cop, like a good soldier, learns how the enemy thinks," he'd said into the phone. "Gotta know their language to defeat 'em."

"No," the woman said. "I am . . . away from my group."

"You're in Arizona. Not Texas. El Paso is four hundred miles from here."

"Ay. Díos mio." She held her fingers to her upper lip and

looked to the east. The child grabbed her leg again and she put her hand on his back. When she turned to me there were tears in her eyes.

I led them to the card table inside. The woman sat down, heavily. "Stay here," I said. "I'll be right back."

Some come across hiding in trucks, others through the desert where there's only barbed wire, and others come directly over the corrugated steel wall, twelve feet high and made of used landing pads salvaged from boats that transported troops in Vietnam and World War II. Three days a week me and my partner, Ted, park a mile outside of Bisbee on a stretch of desert scraped bare for visibility and apprehend them, dozens at a time, as they come over the wall.

They come in crowds. They wait until dark to cross the border, but the floodlights set up all along the line create a stark brightness lighter than daytime. Sometimes they gather on the other side in a group of a hundred or more and rush the fence all at once. They look like British soccer fans on ESPN, storming the field. But there are women and children, and everyone carries a shoulder bag or backpack, and jugs of water. Ted and I and the other agents fill up bus after bus, but still most of the illegals get past us. Last year, three hundred fifty-nine of them died of thirst and exposure crossing the desert.

Once I discovered a corpse on my rounds—an old man, gone for at least a week, still wearing a Dallas Cowboys baseball cap.

Another time Ted and I were the first agents on the scene after a rancher found two dead teenagers curled up under a palo verde tree. The boy was shirtless, holding the pregnant girl. Ted had grumbled about extra paperwork and trudged off to gather the possessions they'd left along the path before they collapsed. When he was gone I sat on the hood of the truck and cried into the empty desert. Ted doesn't let these things get to him. I keep quiet during his tirades about wetbacks and the inherent laziness of all people who live in southern regions of the globe ("warm climates breed people without self-discipline"), although I know my silence implies agreement. I won't draw attention to myself. Ted takes his family to Border Patrol Wives' picnics on Saturdays and his kids play soccer and get in fights at school. With him I rely on the same half grin I learned as a teenager to use with my father. It's a good little smile; it lets me guard something, hold something quiet. My father doesn't know Fran isn't just my roommate. His life is black and white, simple. American or Illegal. Normal or queer. Cop or criminal. The complexity that coats my own life is sticky, and yellowish.

Evenings I go home to Fran and we work on the house we're building next to our trailer, on a spot we chose when we bought the property two years ago. Twenty acres of brush and cactus in the middle of a valley, three miles from our own mailbox. The mountains are distant, but nothing is in the way to block our view.

One night last fall we went out to the house after dinner to finish laying the saltillo tile in the master bathroom. It was still ninety-five degrees, and we were in tank tops and cutoff shorts. After the day I'd had, it was a relief to work with my hands. To create a smooth, level floor that one day soon we would walk on every morning. A bucket of grainy grout sat between us and we worked it into the spaces between the tiles.

Fran sat back on her heels and wiped her forehead with the back of her wrist. Curly brown hair laced with gray escaped the bandana she'd tied around her head. She plopped another trowelful onto the tiles and tried to push her sleeve out of the way.

"How was work?" said Fran.

"Sucked."

"More of the same?" She pulled off her rubber glove and shook it over the bucket. Gray clumps fell out.

"Yeah. You know, it's their faces," I said.

"Whose?"

"The kids. They look at me out of the windows of the buses that bring them back. Hand me that little trowel, would you?"

"They look at you?"

"Yeah. Even in the middle of a crisis, the goddamn kids want to sit by the window. They stare at me. They've got dirty faces, and they've been crying, so there are these . . . clean streaks where the tears went."

"Watch it—that little piece there." Fran said. "It's crooked, see?" I tapped on the edge of the tile with the handle of my trowel and it went straight.

"So—" Fran said.

"I just wish the mothers would make them sit on the aisle." Then, stupidly, I cried. "Premenstrosity," I explained to Fran, who answered with a compassionate snort. Or maybe the tears came from early menopause, or the heat, or stress. Fran didn't press me. She always seems to know when a feeling is just emerging and is too wet, still too unformed to label. She just held me until we got too sweaty to touch skin. The grout dried before we could wipe. The next day we had a hell of a time scrubbing it off the surface of the tiles.

I left the Mexican woman in the house and walked quickly over to the trailer. With those kids hanging on her and as exhausted as she was, she wasn't going anywhere, but still I felt uneasy. When I got to the kitchen I grabbed two large glasses from the cupboard and filled them with water from the faucet.

"Honey," I said. "There's been a development."

Fran looked up from mashing the potatoes. I smelled melting butter. Every year at Thanksgiving my father would offer the same quip about potatoes and the Irish, smiling, with a forkful poised before his mouth. If his dear departed grand-parents could have had 'em with as much butter and cream as my mother put in, he'd say, they'd have died of heart attacks instead of starvation.

"What?" said Fran. "What development?"

"Follow me."

I led Fran next door. I gave the woman one of the glasses and put the other one on the table. The woman put the glass to the child's lips, who drank sloppily, then to the baby's.

Fran approached the child, got down on her knees and looked straight at him. "Tienes hambre?" Are you hungry? The child gave a tiny nod. Fran looked up at the mother. "Ustéd tambien?"

"Fran," I said.

"What?" It was a challenge, though, not a question.

"No," said the woman. "We need to go now."

"Where?" said Fran. "There's nowhere to go. We're twenty miles from anywhere." Fran's Spanish is better than mine. She learned on the job, from all the kids who come through her classroom. "This child—" Fran put her hand on his shoulder, "is too tired to walk another step."

"Fran? Just a minute. Hold on. Can I talk to you? Outside?"

The temperature was starting to drop and Fran stood with her arms wrapped around her middle.

"I'll take them to the checkpoint at Naco right now," I said.

"You wouldn't be back for an hour and a half. Dinner will be ready in twenty minutes."

We looked into each other's eyes, and Fran didn't flinch.

"We can't feed them, Frannie."

"Why?"

"You know why. It's my job. I need to bring them in."

"It's Thanksgiving, goddammit. They're hungry, Mary Pat! The children—"

"Stop it. Just don't."

"Fine. But you know what's going on. You see this every day. Sweetheart, can't you drop the agent thing for a few hours? Just drop it. Let's feed them, for Christ's sake. When dinner's over you'll bring them in. Send them back with full stomachs."

So we set extra places at the table. Like in Andy Griffith, Fran became Aunt Bea, sending a plate of chicken and biscuits over to the jail for Otis. Wednesday nights my father used to pull me onto the couch next to him and we'd eat pretzels and watch our shows, just the two of us. I'd sneak sideways looks at him laughing.

The baby stayed in the cloth sling and the woman coaxed bits of mashed potato into its mouth with her fingers.

"Where's your family?" said Fran. "The children's father?"

"In Chiapas," the woman said. Her name was Maria, and she told us that her husband had fallen ill a week before they were due to leave, together, and if she didn't make the trip they'd have lost the money they'd already paid the coyote. It had taken a year to save it. "So I left," she said, "with the children. We were going to meet in El Paso as soon as he saves enough for the trip. His uncle lives there."

"Your husband, he just let you go?" Fran said. I watched her eyes take in Maria's frayed jeans and the holes in the baby's socks.

"There was no choice." She looked directly at Fran, and I thought we might hear the woman's story then, and within it the story of the children with their faces in the bus windows, but the baby began to fuss.

Fran turned to the child. His name was Martín, and he was mostly eating her stuffing.

"You like it?" she asked.

The boy looked at her seriously, his mouth full, and nodded.

"He has not eaten American food before," said Maria.

"You like our Thanksgiving dinner?" Fran tried English with the boy, a little too loudly.

"He doesn't understand you, Frannie," I said.

His mother spoke. "No, is good. We speak English now. Martín," she addressed the boy. "Say 'Yes.' Say 'Thank you.'"

He looked at his lap.

"Maria," I said, changing back to Spanish, "I need to ask you a question. Are you afraid to go back? Is your life in danger?"

"You mean the fighting in Chiapas. No. My husband and I, we are not involved."

I turned to the window. The sun had slipped behind the mountains and the color had all but faded from the sky. We'd missed the sunset.

Maria helped us carry the dishes back to the trailer. "I have a little money," she said. "If you let me use your telephone I will pay you. I need to call my husband's uncle. He will know what to do."

I ignored the feel of Fran's eyes on me and said, "I'm sorry. I can't let you do that. I need to take you and the children to Naco now."

"Where's that? Is it near El Paso?" Maria rocked her torso in a way that mothers do without thinking, a small bouncing motion.

"No. It's near the border. It's where the immigration checkpoint is."

The woman pulled Martín close to her knees again. "La Migra? Why?" But from the way she stood, from the way she rocked the baby, from the way she didn't look at me but instead at Fran, it was clear she knew why.

"Mary Pat works for the Border Patrol, Maria. It's her job," Fran said, and I was relieved, oddly, as if I don't have to deliver this news to people every day of my life.

"We have come so far. We have spent our money."

"I'm sorry, Maria," I said. I'd never apologized to someone I was about to detain. "Like she said, it's my job."

Fran stood with her backside leaning on the kitchen sink, her arms folded across her stomach. Once, an injured redtail hawk got tangled in our hammock and Fran told me I was crazy to want to pay the vet two hundred dollars to set its wing. She had stood in that spot and argued that we couldn't save every living thing on our property that gets into trouble.

"Let's have some dessert, okay?" she said. "Then you'll go." She pulled the pumpkin pie off the cooling rack near the window.

"Frannie. Stop now," I said.

The boy tugged at his mother's arm and she leaned down to hear his whisper. "May we use your bathroom?" she asked.

When we heard the bathroom door close behind Maria and the boy, Fran said, "She's so proud. And beautiful, don't you think?"

"Christ, Fran. Don't make this hard," I said.

"This is already hard. Whatever I do or say has nothing to do with it." She turned on the faucet, pulled a frying pan crusty with gravy off the stove and squirted soap on it. She held her mouth firm as she scrubbed and the motions made her cheeks shake.

"You know what I mean. I don't have a choice here."

"Don't give me that bullshit, Mary Pat. Everyone has a choice." The water rushed furiously into the sink.

"If I want to keep my job, I mean. If I want to keep my job I don't have a choice. She said she wasn't afraid."

"What? What does that have to do with it?"

"If she was afraid for her life I could get her processed for asylum."

"You've got to be kidding me." Fran turned off the water. "I don't know how you can keep doing this. I'm getting pretty damn tired of it."

"What the hell is that supposed to mean?"

"You know you can stand this job only because you get to drive around the desert. The reason, though, that you're driving around the desert—"

"What?" I said. "The reason is to protect our border. You know that."

"The reason you drive around the desert has nothing to do

with the border. Or illegal immigrants." She grabbed a dish towel and dried her hands. "It has to do with being alone."

The problem with being with someone for eleven years is there's nowhere to hide. The problem with being with Fran, in particular, is she makes connections. She listens to me say one thing, then, months later, another little thing, and it's as if she stores up a cache of innocuous comments and rolls them together into a medicine ball, then when just the right thing happens, when exactly the right moment arrives between us, she hurls the medicine ball with unflinching accuracy and I end up on my ass, in the middle of the kitchen floor.

Fran's voice was soft, now, and she moved in to place her hand on my neck. "You're protecting some kind of border, all right—"

"But I need to believe in the law I enforce. Otherwise . . ."

"I know," Fran said.

Sometimes Fran gives me too much credit. In that moment I ached for dumb neutrality. My father spent eighteen years as a Boston cop. He had a fierce, single-minded righteousness about the law he was paid to enforce.

"Remember why we moved out here in the first place?" Fran said. "You wanted to be a cop. You wanted to help people. Remember when you saw the ad in the *Globe*? The recruitment ad for the Tucson PD?"

"And if I'd have taken that job, we could never have built the house. You wanted this property, Fran. You said I should check out this job." I leaned over and tightened the faucet, a little too hard. "And now we can't go back. It'd take me four years as a cop to get to the salary I'm making now."

"Hey. The Border Patrol was not my idea. Don't put that on me."

I looked out the window over the kitchen sink and out of habit found the green point of light near the horizon that marked the surveillance balloon, then Orion's belt and the Little Dipper, just an inch or so above the mountains. Mexican husbands don't just let their wives and children go off on a dangerous trip like the one Maria had taken. Three years on the job had taught me enough about the culture to be sure about that. I have learned more than I want to know about these people's lives. I have eavesdropped on stories the illegals tell one another in the back seat of my truck, many of them about the fighting in Chiapas. Just then it occurred to me that maybe they wanted me to hear those stories. Surely Maria knew that to tell me outright she and her kids were in danger if she returned was to admit she and her husband were Zapatista revolutionaries, or sympathizers. I would not form an opinion on that whole thing, the conflict they call a civil war. I am hardly able to know what to do about the conflicts that are my own.

I watched the green light in the sky through that tiny trailer window and knew I'd have made the same choice about remaining silent that Maria had. Ted routinely informs Mexican cops when he thinks one of his detainees is Zapatista. I just kept my eyes on the green light and tried not to think that

Maria's husband probably wasn't sick. He was probably dead, or in prison.

Maria and the children came out of the bathroom. I opened the front door and led them to the pale green truck, parked out back. Fran stood on the porch. Her stance said she wanted to follow along and make another point. It felt strange to me, too, to have our argument interrupted. We usually sat there, together, until it was over. Until we each said everything we needed to say.

I put them in the back seat, behind the wire mesh. When I started the job, Fran discovered that child safety seats weren't part of the equipment in my vehicle so she bought one at Wal-Mart and stashed it in the rear. The fabric has cheerful bunnies and balloons and sits, incongruous, in the back of my truck among faded orange jugs of water, olive green safety gear and a government first-aid kit. Ted gives me shit about it.

We rode in silence, the only car on the straight road as far as I could see across the dark empty desert, until Martín began to cry.

"What's wrong?" I said into the rear view mirror.

"He needs to go to the bathroom."

"I thought he went back at the house."

"He has to go again. It happens when he's nervous."

I pulled over to the side of the road and let Maria and the boy out of the truck. The baby slept, and I resolved to give the car seat to Maria when we got to the checkpoint. She could use it for the bus ride back to Chiapas. I watched Martín's back as he hunched over his pant zipper and urinated on a cactus. He was all concentration. He looked up at his mother, and she spoke a few soft words to him.

I thought about isolation, and about what happens after years of keeping your truths only to yourself. We'd built an extra bedroom in our new house in case a co-worker of Fran's or mine were ever to drop by. When it's done we'll put a few pictures of Fran's family in that room, maybe place a hairbrush on the dresser.

My father never told me his reasons for leaving Ireland. I'd called him yesterday to wish him a happy Thanksgiving and told him about all the arrests we'd been making. He grunted, a sign I took as approval. I felt a thrill, then disappointment that I cared so much what he thinks. I've never admitted it to Fran, but I'd wanted to leave Boston—leave our circle of friends—not for the police job in Tucson but because I needed to go away from the place where my father lives. To remove myself from the complex system of falsities we'd created. It's better to be alone in the desert with the mesquite trees and turtles. Or in my truck, following a smooth straight yellow line toward the horizon.

Maria was on one knee in the dirt talking intently to the boy, and I had an image of myself giving her my coat, handing her a jug of water and the compass I keep in the glove box and telling her about the little sanctuary church in Bisbee, about two hours on foot by a desert trail she'd find just over that hill, a path worn smooth by javelina and mule deer and fellow Mexicans. The priest there would get her on a bus to El Paso.

Maria and the boy came back to the truck and I opened the door. Maria helped Martín into his seat, then with her hand on the door frame she looked into my face. "I cannot go back," she said. "There are no jobs..." She smoothed her hair back and lifted her face to the sky. The stars were abundant and bright. I wondered whether they seemed as plentiful in Mexico.

"And we will go hungry," she finished.

"I'm sorry. There's nothing I can do. I can't do anything." I could hand her the compass and never be caught. But then I'd need to go home and tell Fran what I'd done, and I wasn't ready for the things that would be set in motion. She'd make me talk about the fault line that my incremental choices have been built upon. Then she'd realize she's perched as precariously as I am. Fran doesn't have much patience for unstable structures.

I would not think about Maria and the children any more. Neither would I think about my father and what he would do in my shoes. But a small memory popped free, having jumped the track where, despite my oblivion all these years, it had apparently been running in its quiet, smooth circuit: I was ten years old, crouched in my yellow pajamas outside the swinging door to the kitchen, past my bedtime. I'd heard my father's patrol car pull into the driveway and I hadn't been able to stay in bed. He was home for his dinner break and everything in the world was safe when I could hear his voice.

"Fiona," he was saying to my mother, "I couldn't take him in.

I chased the goddamn Mick through every alleyway in the neighborhood and when I caught up with him he was all scraped up, weepin' for his dear mother back in Ireland. He was a young copy of me as a young man. I told him to be off with himself." I heard my mother kiss his cheek, the rustle of her housedress against his uniform, then the squeak of the oven door as she took out the dinner plate she'd kept warm.

There was anguish in his voice when he told my mother about letting the Irish kid go free. To my young ears it must have seemed as if his pain came from thinking he'd been a weak cop. Maybe, though, it came from an absence of clarity.

When I got home Fran would be sitting on the deck, waiting for me, expecting me to tell her how I'm able to hold so many dimensions together and keep them from creating a hopeless mess. She'd need to know I'm solid. I'd tell her it's all about understanding there's a line in the sand. It's all about being able to keep things straight.

I helped Maria into the truck and closed the door. The road was desert dark, as empty as it should be on an evening a month before winter solstice when the whole world is indoors eating turkey with people they love and they hate.

At the checkpoint, the floodlights made the white adminis-tration trailer and the pale green bus glow against the black sky. Agents stopped cars heading north and shone their flashlights inside. I left Maria and the children in the truck and climbed the steps to the trailer to do the paperwork. I gave it to the offi-cer on duty, a nineteen-year-old named Mike. Stuck to the wall behind his desk was a paper turkey wearing a black Puritan hat with a big silver buckle on it.

I went back outside and helped Maria and the children out of the car.

"Here," I said, unbuckling the car seat. "Take this. For the baby."

"It's no use to me," Maria said, "I don't have a car."

"But for the bus?"

"Why do you give this to me? Why do you care?"

She turned away, shaking her head, as if I wasn't worth the effort of a lecture. They boarded the bus. Maria went down the aisle, past a dozen other detainees, and as I watched her I remembered those bodies lying in the desert. As soon as enough illegals were loaded on the bus, the guys would drive them across to Naco. I crossed the empty, floodlit highway back to my truck, carrying the car seat.

I didn't think about turning around. But my body did it anyway, without me, and there in the bus window was Martín, cheeks dry, waving to me. I waved back.

# My Country Wrong

# Jane Rule

There should always be a reason for going somewhere: a death in the family, a lover, a need for sun, at least a simple curiosity. Even a business trip provides excuse for discomfort, focuses discontent. To explain why I arrived in San Francisco on the twenty-third of December, instead of on the twenty-sixth when I was expected, would be nothing but a list of nonreasons. I did not want anything. It was the least distasteful of the alternatives that occurred to me to fill the hole in a blasted schedule. I don't want to talk about the death of friends, failures of domestic courage, the negative guilt of an ex-patriot. It is probably better to be grieving, tired and guilty in a familiar place. San Francisco is familiar enough, home city as much as I ever had one, growing up American. My great-grandparents died there, still speaking German. My mother went to school there, married there with the knees of her bridesmaids showing in both papers. My father went to war with the Japanese from the Oakland Mole. My brother suffered his adolescence in the bars of old North Beach. And I? I used to have lunch with my grandmother in the Palace Hotel, waffles, and the head waiter poured melted butter into each square. She tried to teach me in Chinatown how to recognize Japs by the look of their feet. I had a godmother who sold shoes at the White House because she was divorced. For the same reason my great-aunt had a boarding house somewhere out on a street that ran toward the park, where once I spent a whole, terrified night pulling paper off the wall next to my bed. Grandfather had a pass through the restricted areas all during the war. A city of uniforms, of hotel dances and breakfasts at the Cliff House. A familiar place.

Now again it is a city of uniforms, and, learning the newest routines of the airport, I was distressed by them, not resigned as I had been at their age. Most of the boys do not wear their uniforms well, being unfamiliar with ties and used to putting their hands in their trouser pockets. My grandfather would have been critical. I only wondered if they were as clumsy with guns.

A bright, salt-smelling day, the first of three. I had no plans. I had written a tentative card to Michael and Jessica, another to Lynn, friends I did not usually see in my funeral and wedding ridden returns. Perhaps I'd see Lawrence. There were half a dozen others. But, of those half dozen, three were on their way to jail. I read that in the *Chronicle* in my slot of a hotel room—

the Hilton, which would take more defensive explanation than is valuable. Lawrence was pleading not guilty to disturbing the peace in an anti-draft demonstration. He was trying to disturb the war, he said. Last time I came home my mother said, while we were still at the airport, "You're not going to get involved in any of these marches, are you, darling? You really don't have time to go to jail." It would have been unseemly of me, surely, having given up my citizenship years ago for positive political reasons, for wanting a vote where I lived.

I don't like being ten floors above ground. In San Francisco, every time I am over three floors up, I have fantasies of riding a mattress to Alcatraz, a journey several of us were in the process of attempting when we were discovered and ordered out of the attic. I don't remember whose attic—perhaps my godmother's. Now I understand it is possible to go to Alcatraz by boat, but visiting an empty prison two days before Christmas has no point when old friends are crowded into newer jails.

I had done my Christmas shopping, but I went out into the summer day. The third floor of the City of Paris hasn't been redecorated since my grandmother shopped there. The White House is gone, and my godmother has died of cancer. People are still meeting under the clock at the St. Francis, a dark place, where old men sit and visit on couches just outside the ladies' room. The bar hasn't changed much since my brother and father had one of their many man-to-boy talks twenty years ago, my brother not knowing what to do with a new hat.

I bought books, *Nat Turner* and *All the Little Live Things*, knowing from the reviews that the one would take the last of my irrational liberal hopes that we'd get through without a massacre, that the other would reconfirm the bitter war between the generations, old men drinking themselves to death in Puritan rage, young men hallucinating in tree houses. Is reading a way of not seeing for myself?

Back at the hotel, the red button on my phone was flashing. I had to read a number of directions before I received two messages, one that Michael had appeared "in person," another that Lynn had phoned. And there was a small, live Christmas tree on the desk, about as tall as the bottle of scotch next to it. No card, but it was an unthreatening, discreet kindness. Outside a bus signaled to turn with a high, repeating whistle.

Dinner with Michael and Jessica: the cab driver believed— because of my foreign clothes and shifting accent?—that I had confused streets with avenues. He gave ethnic reports for each more deteriorating neighborhood we passed through. And finally in the block that should have been Michael's, he wanted to turn back. But I saw that one of the Victorian town houses was embarrassed by a nearly completed front porch. I said to the still very reluctant driver, stopped in the middle of the street, shining his police flashlight up the fourteen feet to the front door, that I wanted to get out. He honked, a thing my father says gentlemen do not do. I suppose ladies are not expected to have horns to honk. There was Michael, hurrying down the uncertain new steps, black hair to his shoulders, his side burns white and winged, the bones of his face sharp, the flesh soft, his eyes permanently crossed, caught in their inward gaze by the driver's flashlight.

"This is the place," I said, money ready.

Michael waved the cab away, honking his voice, tenor, nasal. I saw his velvet shirt, the kind I like to buy for myself in men's shops. Around his neck, hanging by a black shoe lace, was a silver lion's head, not medallion so much as door knocker, Metro Goldwyn Mayer. Michael and I are professional rather than personal friends. It was a formal moment before he showed me the path through hardening concrete up to the unfinished entrance. I had not been to the house before because it was new to them. Jessica waited just the other side of the new wrought-iron gates, framed in stained glass. She is tall, cowboy faced, gentle. We were glad to see each other in this kindness they were offering me.

Other people were there, a couple of close friends in the habit of the place, which is a stage set, room by high-ceilinged room. We went nearly at once to Michael's studio on the second floor to see his new paintings, as thick with oil as relief maps, from photographs and prints of nineteenth-century scientific apparatus and bubble gum cards of the Beatles. They would not be properly dry for a hundred years, and then those small mountain ranges of paint would crack into colors of earlier images, flower into the past, or explode. Michael and I would not be there to see it happen, sharing the generation between the great earthquake and his own.

With drinks that Jessica had brought us, we climbed higher.

The walls of the old house have little plaster left from years of a leaking roof, but paintings have been hammered to the old lathing, crowded together up the huge stairwell and along the corridors. The windows that are not stained glass are hung with ancient materials, shawls, rugs, tapestries. On the third floor we found the children, a boy and a girl in their early teens, long haired, bare footed, dressed in jeans and sweaters. They were sitting on the floor and did not greet us.

"Med," Michael explained. "Meditation. It keeps them off pot and away from liquor."

We went down by the back stairs, which cut across the wall of the first-floor toilet, in use as we passed, and turned into the kitchen, where Jessica was cooking.

"How do you like the house?" she asked.

I did not have to answer because the children, having given us time for our slow descent, came quickly and noisily out of their perch of silence, talking like competing commercials or poems.

"To find out if you had a vision or I had a vision," I said, dated by as well as detached from Ginsberg.

"But it works," North said, friendly now and hopeful.

"If you don't cheat," Sky modified as a way of threatening her brother.

Their odd first names are practical to counteract the pages of their last name in any telephone directory. And North has the arctic eyes of his father, but straight. Sky is still child enough to be all style without distinctive definition. They are not so much

57

badly brought up children as unbrought up. What manners they use have the charm of their own invention.

Charlie came out of the bathroom, looking for his drink.

"Charlie doesn't even hold it," North said. "The greatest aim in the west."

Jessica was giving us all things to carry into the dining room, where uncertain chairs were randomly placed at a large, round table. Michael and Jessica sat side by side. The rest of us took places we chose or where we found ourselves. Charlie, between the children, took their hands for a moment. It might have been some sort of grace.

"It's a small table now that everyone's in jail," Sky said.

"And you think everybody over eighteen should be in jail," Charlie said. He was obviously over eighteen but not by very many years. "You're a very uncool person, Sky."

"Is it embarrassing to be out of jail?" I asked.

"Yes," Michael said. "It's so easy for me to stay out."

"I'm going when I'm eighteen," North said. "If they get Charlie."

"They're not going to get me," Charlie assured him. "As soon as I get my degree, I'm going to Canada."

"Maybe you won't have to go," Jessica said. "Maybe nobody will."

"Dr. Spock's going to jail," Sky said.

"He's a very uncool man," Charlie answered her.

"What about Lawrence? What about Joan Baez? And her mother? One of my teachers goes to jail every weekend."

"Well, what does one do?" Michael asked. "Even Jessica read Spock when she was scared. He didn't intend to raise a generation of murderers."

"They're building concentration camps for Negroes and draft dodgers," North said. "They're going to evacuate all of Oakland."

"We're going with them," Sky said. "When the time comes."

"Why doesn't somebody teach these kids to be cool? The country's a jail already. You don't have to go anywhere."

I tasted Jessica's bland food, as gentle and vague as her face, and felt the chair under me give slightly. The children were talking now about a college president who was on probation for refusing to let police turn tear gas and dogs against students who were not rioting. Jessica kept saying to each new threat, "Maybe it won't happen. Maybe you won't have to," which was surely how North was conceived, how she married, how she came to live in this whimsical fortress, continually singing hopeful little unrealities to her cross-eyed husband and her children. Nobody ever encouraged her. Nobody ever said, "No, maybe it won't, Jessica. Maybe we won't have to." Nobody believed her because Jessica was basically one of Charlie's uncool people who had been to jail on principle and off principle until Michael found her and kept in mind what could happen and stopped her. If she was less interesting now than she had been in the days of McCarthy purges and the first UN delegation, she was herself safer in a less safe world.

Some time between the main course and dessert, the chair I

was sitting on disintegrated. After Charlie and Michael helped me up, the children counted eighteen pieces which they carried in to the fireplace in the living room where another bundle of sticks which had also been a chair waited to be burned.

I keep not mentioning Alice. At first I thought she was with Charlie. Then it seemed to me that she might live in the house. She did not say very much. She kissed one or another of the familiar company now and then, more affectingly when she chose Jessica, who obviously liked to touch her since she was of sweeter, safer substance than the rest of us. Or that would have been my reason for liking to touch her. After dinner she read some poems to us, not clearly her own though she did not disclaim them. They were as diffusely erotic as she was and might have been written for her. The children meditated in various, undisciplined postures, until they fell asleep, in random touch with one or another adult. We were free then to talk of things other than draft dodging, race riots, and drugs. Michael wanted to talk about photographs, those fixed hallucinations from which he worked. Near him was a portrait he had done of old Mrs. Winchester from a photograph, not looking frightened of the things she was frightened of. On his lap was a box of photographs of himself as a child, of machines, of boxers, of Alice, to whom I looked for some explanation. There was none.

At midnight, Charlie drove me back to the Hilton with only a trace of embarrassment, and I invited him to visit me as I always invite people to visit. My phone was flashing with new messages, and there was no direction for stopping it without receiving them.

In the morning, I had Christmas cards with foreign postmarks, and out in the bright day a Salvation Army band played by a place advertising topless lunches. In the dining room an Hawaiian tour had just arrived, fifty dyspeptic grandparents with midwestern accents, stricken with pleasures they would rather have read about than paid for. One couple had apparently missed the plane, but they were there somehow, moving from table to table relieving people with their simple anger.

San Francisco is not a beautiful city, except at the distance from it I usually keep. From Berkeley, from Sausalito, from nearly anywhere else, even the sky, it is white and as abruptly mountainous as one of Michael's paintings. But in the city are the centers of pretentious civic architecture, green domes and irrational spires among a cluttered, dwarfed, bay-windowed suburbia. I went to the parks, to the museums, to the cliffs above the Golden Gate, that narrow channel of catastrophes. Across it was a military installation on a golden winter hill with a large, outlined Christmas star for night shining. I went to Cost Plus and bought Korean brass and postcards from Vietnam.

Dinner with Lynn: Christmas Eve is not a time to go out for dinner; so many French, Italian, and Mexican restaurants shut. Lynn came to the hotel, dressed in a carefully tailored suit, stiff-collared blouse and cameo where a tie might have been. Soft-haired, soft-spoken, amusement and surprise always faint in her face. We had a drink in the hotel while we decided where to go. The exposed thighs of our forty-year-old waitress were not appetizing. Still, we had another drink.

"If we have to choose," Lynn said, "I'd rather have tits."

"Not for dinner. There must be an unbelieving Mexican or Frenchman somewhere in the city."

There was, in Ghirardelli Square. We walked through the shops first, stepping over clay hens and carp, barnacled with succulence, looking at nests of bright boxes, primary colors everywhere. At a shop for child art, a woman was handing out pamphlets for the protection and support of the imagination. The drawings and paintings on display were obviously teacher chosen, either psychiatric or rigid with the right ideas, but occasionally a child had been willfully childish: a tall house among giant flowers, a sun round in the corner, every object with a face, a bright face. Out in the square itself all the Christmas lights were white, a relief.

We ordered guacamole with a third martini, drank and watched the traffic under and across the bridge. Then we ate the hot food that reminded me of country fairs and my grandmother's cleaning woman, depression food in expensive surroundings. Lynn will not talk unless she is asked questions. I ask questions, thin and general, because I don't know much about efficiency engineering.

"I'm all right now, but there's less and less space to move."

"Why?"

"Nearly everything is war industry."

"And you don't want to work in war industry?"

"Oh, I don't care about that. Simply being alive is murderous. Beyond that, moral choice is a theoretical exercise. The point is I can't work in war industry. I can't get security clearance."

"Why not?"

Lynn smiled with derisive sweetness.

"Is it that bad?"

"When the security people come to ask me about friends I had in graduate school, they ask two questions: is he homosexual and has he ever been to a psychiatrist."

"They wouldn't stop someone who'd been to a psychiatrist," I said.

"I don't know, but there are a lot of people who think it's pretty risky to go to one."

"It's getting very bad," I said.

"I think about getting out, going to Canada, but there's not much for me yet in Canada."

"I suppose not."

"Never mind. I'm having a lovely time. Most people are. A lot of money and a taste of illegality in nearly everything takes care of it."

There is no point ever in arguing with Lynn. Ideas for her are no more than wry confessions. To debate failures of conscience is inappropriate. She paid for my dinner, and we went out to find her car, which I would have been impressed by if I knew anything about cars. I knew only that much. We drove over the hills and out to the Haight-Ashbury district.

"The flower children are almost gone," Lynn said. "There are a couple of good bars."

I was not properly dressed, being properly dressed, in navy silk with a green silk coat. I have other kinds of clothes, even a pair of modest boots, which I would have been glad of, but in whatever costume I would have to carry my age. It becomes me, defining and refining a person out of the blur of adolescence, but persons are troublesome in the places Lynn wanted to go. She's eight years younger than I, the acceptable side of thirty.

As we walked down a quiet side street, we could hear people singing Christmas carols in an apartment above us. One hundred miles to the south, my family had gathered for the same purpose: parents, brother, sisters, nieces and nephew decorating a tree. I had not gone home for Christmas for fifteen years. Only deaths and marriages. My arrival on the twenty-sixth would be without excuse, no relative left to say goodbye to, my parents settled in the static status of the sixties, in my own generation first and even second marriages achieved, the new generation still being measured in steps and inches.

The bar was so crowded that at first we didn't realize we had walked into a Christmas Eve party. Not only all the bar stools and chairs had been taken, but it was difficult to move through the clusters of standing people. A huge man, probably the only man in the place, dressed in a Santa Claus suit, handed us chits for free drinks.

"The bouncer," Lynn explained.

She went to get us drinks, leaving me to occupy what space I could find. I moved farther into the room where a pool table had been covered, obviously ready for food. Only a few people leaned against it; so I joined them without being friendly. On a wall near the juke box was a sign which read, "Pool Table Reserved for Ladies and their Guests." Eight or nine couples were trying to dance, youngsters most of them, some in stylish hip-hugging trousers and nearly transparent shirts, others in earnest drag, everything from conservative business suits to motorcycle outfits. They were having fun. It felt like a party, and I was smiling vaguely at it by the time Lynn got back. She had two college students with her, one tall sulky girl in a very well-tailored slack suit whose name was Ann, one short dandy with cropped curly hair, a pin-striped suit out of the thirties, and a cigarette holder. She wanted Lynn to dance, so Ann and I held drinks and braced ourselves against the table.

"Tourist?" she asked.

"Not really."

I hadn't been in this kind of bar since my own college days when I was a tourist, but not simply in this world—in all worlds of social definition. Now, careful to have unoffending costumes for most circumstances, I was still, as a traveler, often caught in the wrong one.

"Lynn said you wouldn't want to stay."

"I'm traveling," I said. "I haven't much time."

It was too noisy to talk anyway; so we drank our drinks, then drank the ones we were holding for the other two, and watched the crowd. I was putting my second glass down on the pool table when Ann put an arm around my shoulder. It startled me until I realized why she had done it. A motorcycle rider, nearly as tall as the bouncer, heavy set and handsome, was approaching us.

"Taken?" she said to Ann.

"An old friend from out of town," Ann said carefully.

The explanation was acceptable apparently. The cycle rider nodded and moved on.

"We'd better dance," Ann said.

I hadn't been on a dance floor for perhaps ten years, but only a few of these dancers shook themselves and stared at their own feet. Most of them liked the public declaration of being in each other's arms. I could dance the way I was being asked to. The novelty of it for me, the grace and protectiveness of my partner, were new pleasures. Once I caught sight of Lynn, watching, with that characteristic faintness of surprise and amusement, and I wondered what kind of fool I was making of myself. It was difficult to determine. I am not used to this kind of attention and protection. If dancing had occurred to me, I would have expected to ask.

"Drink?" Ann suggested.

"May I buy it?"

She looked down at me, obviously calculating what that would mean, ready to be agreeable.

"Just to buy it," I said. "I can't stay long."

"Then I'll buy it."

"Like?" Lynn asked, free for a moment from her dandy.

"She's sweet," I said, "but I can't stay around being a hazard."

"What makes you think you're a hazard?"

"These clothes. This age I haven't any business letting kids cake care of me."

"Why not? She wants to. She'd like you to stay."

"How often do you come here?"

"A couple of times a week, I guess."

The questions I hadn't asked at dinner could not be asked now. Still I began to ask.

"Why? What's happened to Jill?"

"She got married last year," Lynn said, "to a very good security risk."

"Still ..."

"Let's stay another hour, all right?" Lynn interrupted. She had just seen someone she obviously wanted to see. "Then we'll go if you like."

The girl Lynn greeted was with someone else. The tension was unpleasant.

"You don't really like it here do you?" Ann said, handing me a drink.

"It's a very good party. Thank you."

"We could go some place else."

Lynn was dancing

"Who is that?" I asked.

"The one with Lynn? I don't know ... any more. She used to be a friend of mine. Why did you let Lynn bring you here? And why is she embarrassing you like this?"

"She's not," I said. "We're old friends."

"That's all?"

"That's all."

"I didn't know anything was like that any more. Let's dance."

This time it was not easy to do. There was something wrong between Lynn and Ann, a competitiveness.

"We're going down the street for a quiet drink," Ann said to Lynn. "We'll be back in about an hour."

"Why don't I call you at the hotel?" Lynn said, obviously wanting to be helpful.

"All right," I said. Out on the street, I said to Ann, "Let's find a cab for me, and you go back to the party."

But she was hurt; so I walked along with her until we found a bar that was not having a party. I had already had enough to drink, and so had she. I wondered if she was twenty-one.

"I want plain soda," I said.

"Two plain sodas."

"Why are you by yourself on a Christmas Eve?" I asked.

"Why are you?"

"An error in the schedule," I said. "That's all. It happens when you travel a lot."

"I didn't want to go home."

"Well, neither did I, I guess."

"You aren't gay, are you?"

It's an unanswerable question from my point of view, but I am more often than not doubtful about my point of view.

"Yes," I said, regretting it.

"Then why are we sitting here?"

Why? Because I hadn't the sense to know what mood Lynn was really in, what trouble she was in. Because I had on the wrong clothes. I was also wearing the wrong manners, hetero-sexual, middle-aged manners which involve so many frankly empty gestures.

"We're sitting here because I don't know what else to do."

"I don't understand."

"I know you don't. Shouldn't I take a cab before I begin to give you motherly advice out of sheer embarrassment? I haven't been in that kind of bar since I was your age—fifteen … twenty years ago? It's no time for me to begin. And, as for you, you're not supposed to trust anyone over thirty."

She smiled then, for the first time, and I relaxed a little until she said, "But I think older women are wildly attractive."

"I do, too."

"Oh."

"But not in bars," I went on. "I like them in their own living rooms or on lecture platforms or in offices. I've never danced with one."

"I was only trying to be polite," Ann said.

"I know, and I'm touched by it, but there isn't any way to be polite to me."

"I don't want to go back there either," she said. "Let me stay with you, just for the evening. We could go to a movie or just drive around or go back to my apartment."

Christmas Eve: I should have been in my own apartment

cooking a turkey or at home eating one. Or I should have, given all the wrong choices so far, found Lynn and made her take me home to hers. For her own sake, but she did not want to go. Ann and I walked back to the party to make sure. Then we walked again to find Ann's car. I did not want to stay in these remnant crowds, the dying market of flowers. We drove to North Beach and walked in Chinatown. I suppose the shops have always been full of dull, dirty jokes, but I looked for the miniature worlds I loved when I was a child, not stocking presents for the tired and impotent. At midnight, when we might have been in church, we were in my hotel room, drinking scotch, I in the chair by the window, Ann stretched long on one of the beds.

"I'm essentially a very uncool person," she said.

I yawned, thinking of Charlie.

"Merry Christmas," she said.

"Merry Christmas."

I got up to pour a last drink, saw Ann watching me in the mirror, and felt guilty. It did not very much matter to me what I did on this particular evening. At her age, I would have wanted very badly whatever I wanted.

"I feel like a bouncer in Santa Claus disguise," I said.

"You don't have to throw me out. I'll go."

I sat down on the bed beside her. She didn't move. I put a hand on her thigh, and she turned a little toward me, but she did not reach out. I was, for a moment, surprised, then relieved into having to give more than permission. She wanted me as I am used to being wanted by a woman ... never mind that length of body, the boyish manners. I wanted to laugh, to tease her, but I was afraid to. Her body was so young under my hands, her need so seriously sacred. I was afraid, too, that she would come to me before I had even undressed her or that she would not come at all if moved too slowly. I had to be very careful, very gentle, control the comic wonder I felt in myself, wanting not simply to be good in bed out of thoughtful habit but to be marvelous at once. But she was as understated and as graceful as she had been on the dance floor, leading only to invite being led, if I had noticed, if I had wanted to notice. She came to me perfectly at the moment I wanted her to.

"You did want me."

"Apparently," I said, and then I did laugh, surprised by her immediate and confident change of mood.

"You wear such pretty clothes."

I am not either twenty or practiced in adjusting my own desire to strangers. The few experiences of this sort that I have had in the last ten years have always embarrassed me and, to some extent, made me feel guilty. I don't believe in fidelity, though it is for me the only practical way to live.

"Don't do that," Ann was saying to me. "Don't go away from me like that."

"I'm sorry."

I must have natural bad manners in bed. I had also had too much to drink. I drifted toward her touch for a moment, enjoying it, then drifted away near sleep.

"I'm sorry," she said.

"How old are you?"

"Eighteen."

"You ought to go home," I said.

Once she had, I couldn't sleep. I read until seven in the morning, ordered breakfast in my room, then took *All the Little Live Things* up to the roof and sat in seventy degrees of sun by an empty swimming pool until a woman joined me who wanted to know if I thought the deck chairs at the Athens Hilton weren't better than these.

"I haven't been to the Athens Hilton."

"The chairs are better. I have trouble with my back."

I turned a page.

"They ought to be all the same. It's a chain, after all."

I closed my book and took the elevator to the lobby. There was a telegram. I sent a reply and then walked up the street to *David's* for lunch, lox and cream cheese. When I paid the bill, the cashier handed me a small box. Out on the street, I opened it to find four large macaroons and the message, "Eat thy macaroons with joy. David."

I went back and bought two dozen macaroons. Then I went to my room, closed my suitcases and phoned my brother. He would meet the bus.

And say "How's the picture business, Sis?" or "Mother's worried there aren't enough sweet potatoes," or "It's like you to be the only goy at *David's* on Christmas day." It's a long ride on the Bay Shore which has tabled out over the years so that there are no landmarks left, forests or hills of flowers, nothing except occasional hangars, faint structures in the haze.

What he did say was, "I think I'm going to Vietnam next week."

Christmas dinner at home.

"They give them estrogen, that's all. When they're about eight or nine. They stop growing and start developing. And if it's a matter of having to wear a bra in the fifth grade or go through life six feet tall ..."

"Harry sent off to Charles Atlas and got this questionnaire about whether or not he was popular. 'Are you constipated?' 'Do you have bad breath ...'"

"Charles Atlas must be one hundred and two."

"Aren't you proud of your brother going off to Vietnam? They'll only send him where it's safe, of course, just where the President goes."

"Friends of ours won't even take a plane that flies *over* France."

"It's easier to share a crust of bread than a feast, that's why. I mean, if all you have is a crust of bread, who cares?"

"I showed the cops where I found it—a whole great big sack of it, just sitting in a tree. I was looking for snakes."

"People with long hair want to go to jail."

"She said all the men who go to concerts are queer. I said, 'Well, George isn't.' She's just jealous."

"Every year I think I like the pink camelia best until the white one comes out, and then I just can't make up my mind."

"Why decide?"

"I like to know what I like."

"If you want to know what I think, I think Charles Atlas is dead."

"Then who's reading his mail? That's illegal."

"Look, a bra in the fifth grade is an asset. Ask Harry."

"I think saying grace in Latin is phoney. God speaks English, doesn't He?"

"We learned *Jingle Bells* in Latin."

"It's going to be a long war, that's all."

"Is the turkey dry?"

"Not the dark meat. I suppose you're used to goose."

"Poets live in trees."

"Don't argue about it; discuss it."

They all have names, and I have no trouble remembering them. In fact, I say their names too often when I'm talking to them. I have loved the children, each one. But Harry, the oldest, my brother's son, is most familiar to and with me. He invited me to see the workout room he was digging out under the garage. And, while I stood, admiring the hole in the ground, he took off his jacket, tie and shirt, and reached for his pick axe. I watched the easy rhythm of his young muscles, the sun on his California color hair. He hadn't been at work for more than five minutes when I looked up to see a girl sitting on the stone fence, then another in the apple tree. They perched as still as birds.

"How old are you, Harry?"

"Nearly old enough," he said seriously.

Mother was calling from across the yard. "It's long distance, dear."

I never have any trouble deciding for the white camelia.

"That isn't what 'homesick' means exactly," I said into the phone. "Yes, sell it." And then to the question of how long I would be away, "Long enough to say goodbye to Harry."

It shouldn't have come as a surprise.

"Oh, screw the kids," my brother was saying. "It's Christmas and I want another drink."

Charles Atlas isn't dead; it's the children who are mortal. Now that grandparents are all dead, now that everyone who is going to marry has married, it is time to say goodbye to the children. I came home to say goodbye to North and Sky and Ann and Harry.

# JANEBISHOP'S EYES

## Valarie Watersun

Children chortled with laughter as they stomped and shouted a welcome to winter's first snowfall.

"A white Christmas," Reed muttered, one hand swatting at a drifting snowflake.

She had been watching the playing children for quite a while and they were beginning to eye her with some alarm. After all, it was cold and here she was, standing in the doorway, no coat, not even a sweater, just a faded Florida Everglades T-shirt. The shirt had been a hot, flamingo pink once, in its heyday. Now it offered little, not even protection against the weather. She was also letting cold air into the apartment, increasing a heating bill that she couldn't afford as it was. Nevertheless, she lit another cigarette, letting it droop from her lips so she could shove her numb hands into the front pockets of her jeans. A passerby would think her hunched due to the cold but in all truth it was despair that curved her form. She pulled on the cigarette enjoying satisfaction as a snowflake sizzled in the glowing ember. Pale blue smoke escaped her lips and ventured into the still winter air. She watched it disperse and her heart ached from its angelic, tentative beauty.

It was pure folly taking her eyes off Karen's kids, however, for one of them let fly a big garbageball and it slapped into the door frame showering her with tidbits of ice and gravel. Although she hadn't witnessed the attack, she knew it had been implemented by Sonny because he was first to take cover, giggling his victory.

She glowered meanly, as was expected, and turned to move inside. A chorus of "Aw, come on, Reed, it was only a joke," followed her, so, delighting them, she flashed her middle finger and closed the door on their raucous laughter.

Crossing before the large foyer mirror Reed had to pause and look twice at her reflection. Seeing herself fast like that—with little detail—was like seeing her twin sister Cory and it always gave her a shock. Not so much because Cory was dead—from a biking accident several years ago—but rather because what right did Reed have to live on when beautiful, sweet-natured Cory was dead?

Her lips twitched as she stared at her reflection and she recognized the craving: vodka. Her old friend vodka always eased the ache.

Even cutting her hair short—military short—hadn't lessened

the resemblance to Cory. Cory's eyes watched her, Cory's lips twitched, craving the booze that until eighteen months ago had been Reed's life. She missed it, every day, but didn't miss the puking or that constant urgency to find the next bottle. She'd given all that up, thanks to the program and, yeah, to JaneBishop.

It was always said like that. It was never just Jane or just Bishop but JaneBishop, one word said real fast. Reed, with her butch camaraderie, had tried to shorten it to JB but Jane Bishop had set her straight fast enough. JaneBishop, she'd said firmly. It's JaneBishop. Reed could hear her voice even now; straightforward. To the point.

She's gone. The thought hit Reed hard, much harder and more direct than Sonny's garbageball. She felt her throat begin to swell with the knowledge and quickly pulled in anger to replace it.

"Bitch," Reed spat out, scolding an empty house. Passing into the living room, she stared angrily at the huge Christmas tree JaneBishop had insisted on having. It had cost Reed an entire day's pay but it had been okay then.

"The tree or my undying love," Reed had teased. They had braved frigid wind looking for a small, economical tree and found this beauty instead. And JaneBishop had smiled at Reed, pink face peering from around the tree's girth, eyes twinkling from a mysterious inner merriment that Reed could never hope to comprehend. "I'll take both," she'd replied, her hand seeking Reed's hand, her voice low and sexy. "I'm greedy."

The memory caused another flare of pain and anger. "Greedy is right," Reed told the tree. "She just had to go shake that old money bag, didn't she?" The tree didn't answer although its sparse covering of white lights whispered quietly, like JaneBishop's eyes.

Reed turned her favorite chair so it faced away from the tree. She sat in it carefully as if moving too suddenly might shatter the framework of bitterness and fury she was building.

It wasn't fair. Just because someone is lesbian is no reason for hate. Yet JaneBishop's mother hated Reed. Had even barred her from the Eastside garden apartment where she lived. And that was just okay by Reed because it was a pigsty anyway. Reed and JaneBishop didn't have much but what they did have was clean as soap. Reed saw to that personally. JaneBishop's mother would never know it though, would never lower herself to come to this part of town. Even if Reed were to grow her hair back long, Mrs. Quince would still mark her as queer and out to corrupt her daughter. This was nothing new, hell, people had known about Reed since grade school. She just had that way about her, no matter how she tried to conform to the het world. And mannerisms from two years in St. Mary's Reformatory for Young Women for a B & E just added fuel to the fire. As did the half-moon of scar on her right cheek, relic of a battle for dominance her first week in prison. True, she was no prize but then neither was JaneBishop or JaneBishop's mother. They were no better than anyone else. Mrs. Quince was a mean alcoholic who lay in bed until midday every day, living on her dead husband's life insurance policy and feeling like it gave her the okay to run JaneBishop's life. She had some nerve, giving Reed grief.

And JaneBishop, the traitor, right up in there, sucking on the old tit so she could inherit some day. Didn't she realize that Reed wanted to take care of her? Forever? Reed pressed her lips together and made a steeple of fingers that wanted to clench in frustration. She pushed the tip of the steepled fingers into her chin, the pain helping focus thoughts that wanted to collapse into a chaos of ache.

The fight had been pretty bad. The worst of their two-year relationship. Reed shouldn't have been so hard about JaneBishop's mom. It was Christmas after all. JaneBishop had every right to visit her mother. That's what people did on holidays. Just because Reed had no family left didn't mean JaneBishop had to deny hers.

But JaneBishop was Reed's family, her only family, and she wanted desperately to be JaneBishop's family in return. Couldn't JaneBishop see that? Reed didn't have the words to make her realize it, either. Not when she was angry like that, when all she could say was hurtful things she didn't even mean. Like how JaneBishop was a money-grubber—out for Dad's little piece of life insurance. Reality painted a very different picture and Reed wasn't the one blind to it. She knew JaneBishop wasn't that way.

No one knew JaneBishop as well as she did.

She thought of other times, quiet times lulled by the glow of lovemaking. Reed could talk then. They could talk then. And they shared all the secrets of their personal worlds; they told each other about the fears that stymied them, the uncertainty that plagued them, and the dreams that comforted them. She remembered how they held one another, like two embryos, trapped together in a womb of separation from the outside world, buffered from the harshness of their daily lives. They needed one another, the codependence of their alcoholism just a small portion of the whole. Apart they became inanimate limbs torn from a host body. Together they could cohere and move forward.

A sigh struggled through Reed's chest, and eyelids fatigued from forcing back tears drooped across her vision. How could JaneBishop leave like that? After all they'd meant to one another? Leaving Reed on Christmas Eve was an unforgivable blow. People were drinking, partying. Didn't JaneBishop realize how easy it would be for either of them to have that one little drink that would dump them right off the wagon into frigid December snow? Reed licked her lips and laid her smoldering cigarette in the ashtray. She could go out drinking if she wanted to. It wasn't as if anybody cared anymore. JaneBishop was probably snorting back the big one with her mom, just like old times. Although she tried to envision her lover drinking with Mom Quince, the image just wouldn't jell. Instead she saw JaneBishop making her way carefully around the sunny kitchen of their apartment, watering the dozen or so plants that she just had to have. She'd buy them little, just because they smelled good and then they'd take off and grow for her and become huge, feathery hugs for her to enjoy every morning.

Mornings would be the worst, Reed thought ruefully as she drifted into sleep, dreaming about a life without JaneBishop. Coming awake, she placidly watched the reflection of the tree lights in a naked corner of living room window. The lights sparkled just like JaneBishop's green eyes.

Hours later Reed woke to a cold house. She hated to fall asleep with no blanket, to awaken chilled to the bone. She had a shaking urge for a hot bourbon toddy, with lemon and a pile of wet sugar in the bottom of the glass. And sighed. Would the urge for booze ever leave? "It's just a habit," she said aloud as she gained her feet and made her way to the kitchen. She leaned over the cracked enamel sink and drank a big glass of the tepid city water. It was just fine.

The silence of the house crept over her. It felt like the empty socket left after a wisdom tooth has been pulled, hollow and aching. Walking back toward the living room, she saw something sparkling on the wooden floorboards. Crouching down, she tried to pick it up but the ice crystal imploded as soon as her finger touched it. Lifting the wet fingertip, Reed frowned in puzzlement then noticed that there was a trail of wetness and ice. Following it, she allowed excitement to nibble at her heart.

She saw the draping of blue as soon as she rounded the door frame. JaneBishop sat on the floor against the boughs of the tree, her blue poncho trailing along the floor like a distorted Christmas tree skirt. Her red shirt was a good contrast against the green tree and the colors made Reed think of the soldier in the Nutcracker ballet. Reed wanted to say so much, but found the words locked in her throat. Then she saw the bottle propped between JaneBishop's legs and was too afraid to talk.

"Reed?" JaneBishop said softly.

"Yeah, babe," Reed answered quickly, knowing how her partner hated being ignored when someone else was in the room. "It's me. What you got there?" Reed knew exactly what it was. Scotch, J&B by the distinctive label. She could almost taste it, it was so familiar.

JaneBishop sighed. She sounded so tired and discouraged that Reed's eyes filled up with tears. "Just booze," she replied, preoccupied by thought, her voice distant. "From Mama's."

"Are you drinking it?"

JaneBishop turned and her wobbling gaze almost fixed on Reed. "No. I was going to and I opened it. I smelled it and you know what?"

"What?" Reed settled herself on the floor at JaneBishop's feet, laying a palm against her leg so she'd know Reed had changed position. The tilt of JaneBishop's head changed, lowered.

"I realized what I really wanted was the smell of your skin."

Reed drew in a huge breath and held it.

"I hated being at Mama's without you. She's not like you, not good like you are. She is so miserable and hates her life." She leaned forward. "Do you realize how very wonderful our life is together?"

Reed allowed the air to escape her lungs. Tears broke free and cascaded along her scarred cheek. "Oh yeah, babe. Yeah. I do."

"I'm sorry I left. I'm sorry I got so mad. Can you forgive me?"

Reed had buried her face in the hard convexity of her knees and her voice was muffled, choked off. "Done, honey, that's all done," she chanted.

JaneBishop remained silent and lilting Christmas music from the house next door filled the room with faint cheer. Reed reached out and grasped JaneBishop's hand. They sat that way a long time, through *O Tannenbaum* and *Jingle Bells*.

"Let's get rid of this," JaneBishop said finally, indicating the bottle. "I don't think either of us needs it."

"You got that right," Reed agreed, helping pull JaneBishop to her feet. She used the toe of her right sneaker and expertly flipped JaneBishop's cane from the floor into her hand. She passed it to JaneBishop and moved around so JaneBishop could take her arm, a graceful dance practiced to perfection long ago. They moved in tandem to the front door and out into the coldness of snow and ice and Christmas. Moving to the porch railing, JaneBishop draped her cane across one arm and used both hands to twist open the bottle. She leaned out into the night and poured the oily essence of scotch into the snow below. "We're anointing the Holly King," she said with a giggle. "How pagan is that?"

"Pagan enough, " Reed said. "Our luck is sure to improve."

JaneBishop turned her face toward Reed and Reed swore for

the thousandth time that she could see her. "I don't think it could get much better, Reed. We're so lucky to have found one another at that AA meeting."

"I love you, sweetheart," Reed said gently, her heated words supplying all the visual stimulus her lover might miss. She moved close so she could hold JaneBishop's face in both palms.

JaneBishop's dark eyes began to twinkle and that old familiar mystery returned. "I told you I was greedy. See, I got the tree and your undying love. Such a good Christmas!"

# X-MAS
## (EX-MESS)

# Zonna

Tracy stared at the small slip of paper as if she'd forgotten how to read. Then she shook her head violently and tried to put the paper back into the coffee can.

"What are you doing?" Gina scolded.

"I have to pick over."

"You can't."

"I have to."

Gina pulled the can out of Tracy's reach. "You can't just keep picking till you get someone you like."

"Why not?"

"Because that would ruin the entire spirit of the Secret Santa tradition."

*Oh, so now it's a tradition . . .* As far as Tracy knew, this was the first year the office had ever done it.

"Who's gonna know? I won't tell if you don't."

"Oh, why don't you just grow up?"

Gina left Tracy's cubicle in a huff and headed for the next contestant.

Tracy crumpled the paper and angrily tossed it into her already overflowing wastepaper basket. Then she quickly retrieved it. Maybe she could trade with someone else. She made a half-hearted attempt to smooth the creases away, then she unplugged her headset from the phone jack and peered over the flimsy partition for a likely victim.

Three desks away, Susan was unfolding a red square.

Tracy waited until Gina moved on before she strolled over to the water cooler, ever so casually. "Hey, Susan."

"Hi, Tracy. These leads are terrible today, aren't they?" Susan held up a pack of index cards.

"Yeah."

"I got four hang ups in a row."

"Yeah, well, maybe it's too early in the morning for people to be thinking about credit cards."

"Maybe."

Tracy made her move. "I see you got your Secret Santa assignment."

Susan smiled. "Forget it, Tracy. Gina warned me you'd try to trade. We're not allowed."

*Damn that Gina!* Ever since she'd been promoted to office manager she'd gone mad with her modicum of power.

"Who'd you get?" Tracy forged forward anyway.

"I can't tell you. It's supposed to be a secret, silly."

"Damn it, Susan! It's not like it's a matter of national security or anything! Who'd you get?"

Susan flinched visibly, then lowered her voice to a whisper. "Mary Anne from accounting."

*Mary Anne* . . . Tracy searched her memory files for a photo. *Oh, yeah—mousy, little blonde* . . . "Trade with me. Please?"

"I can't."

"Come on! What's the big deal? I promise Gina won't find out."

"No." Susan shook her head stubbornly.

Tracy thought for a moment. *Sweeten the pot* . . . "Tell you what—trade with me and I'll give you credit for my next three sales."

Susan hesitated, then folded her arms across her chest. "Absolutely not. I already know what I'm buying for her. Why can't you just play right? Who did you get, anyway?"

Tracy closed her eyes. "Donna."

Susan shrugged. "So? Didn't you two used to be friends?"

"Sort of. Not for a while," Tracy answered, evasively.

"Well, maybe this will be a good chance to patch things up. It *is* the Christmas season, fa la la and all that." Susan smiled a vacant smile and adjusted her headset. "I don't understand why you're so upset. It should be easy. You were close. You know exactly what she likes."

Tracy slumped away.

*What she likes . . . I can hang myself outside her apartment. She'd like that.*

What Tracy couldn't explain to Susan was that she and Donna had been "more than friends." They'd been lovers for almost two years. They'd broken up (for the third and last time) that past June, right in the middle of the local Pride Parade. It hadn't been one of those quiet, amicable splits, either. Come to think of it, nothing about their relationship had ever been what anyone might call either quiet or amicable. Passionate, impulsive, tumultuous—those words were better suited to describe the twenty-three and a half months they'd spent tormenting one another.

Continuing to work in the same office was awkward, but neither could afford to quit. Telemarketing didn't pay much, but it was flexible. And this particular job provided a decent enough salary before commissions, so giving it up was not an easy choice. Besides, neither woman was willing to back down and slink away in defeat. They managed by working different shifts when they could and totally ignoring one another when they couldn't. Not a word had been spoken between them in six months, which was just fine with Tracy's new girlfriend, Marie. She tended to lean a bit toward the jealous side of the street.

Tracy plopped down in her chair and shuffled listlessly through her leads. She plugged herself back into the phone and poked out the first number. Clearing her throat, she practiced pronouncing the name on the card while counting the rings. *One...two...three...four...* "Hello? May I speak to Ellen—Misken—Mitskenschvitz? Yes? Hello, ma'am. Happy holidays. How are you today? That's good. My name is Tracy and I'm calling with a special offer from—Hello? Hello?"

The phone hummed in her ear.

From across the office, Donna's laughter tinkled like a silver bell. Tracy raised the volume on her headset. She turned the card over and moved onto the next one.

"Why don't you just drop out of the whole thing, then?" Karen wiped the crumbs from her fingers with a napkin.

Tracy pushed some food from one side of her plate to the other. "Everyone already thinks I'm a snob."

"Who cares what they think?"

"I do. I have to work with them every day."

"Then just get over it."

"And what am I gonna tell Marie?"

"Tell her the truth."

"She won't believe me."

"Then don't tell her anything."

"Right, and then she'll find out, and it'll look like I was trying to hide something."

"Well, aren't you?" Karen tossed her credit card onto the table.

"How much do I owe you?" Tracy made as if to reach into her pocket, knowing full well that it contained only three singles, two quarters, four pennies and a piece of lint.

"Never mind," Karen offered. "You have bigger things to worry about."

"Thanks for reminding me," Tracy groaned.

"Why don't you just get Donna a CD and be done with it?"

"Because."

"Because why?"

"Just because."

"I don't know why you're making such a big thing about it. It's just a silly little office party."

"You wouldn't understand."

Karen was self-employed. She designed websites from the comfort of her living room. She had no boss, no employees, no girlfriend, and no understanding of what it took to deal with any of the above.

"Guess not," Karen sucked on an ice cube and shrugged.

They left the café and took off in opposite directions. Tracy wandered around the Village for a while, popping into every eclectic shop she passed. She couldn't give Donna something stupid like a CD. She'd slept with the woman, for goodness' sake. Tracy felt as if she had to at least put some thought into it. On the other hand, she couldn't get anything really personal, or Marie would kill her.

*Face it, she'll be pissed no matter what I get. I'm screwed.*

The streetlights were decorated with pine branches, making them look like mutant trees. The cold air smelled like burnt chestnuts. Usually this was Tracy's favorite time of year. She loved skating at Rockefeller Center, walking through Central

Park in the snow; even watching the corny Rockettes' Christmas spectacular. New York in the winter could be magical. This Secret Santa thing was spoiling the whole season for her. She felt like the Grinch. She could feel her lip curling up into a nasty snarl.

All of a sudden, Tracy stopped short. The pedestrian behind her cursed under his breath. She peered into a dingy storefront window, then hurried inside.

"May I help you?" a myopic clerk inquired.

"I wanna buy a music box."

"Well, then you've come to the right place. We have a variety of beautiful wooden boxes, all hand-crafted, of course. And we can load them with any selection from this list, here, on the wall." He pointed to a sheet of paper.

"How much?"

"The prices are on the bottom of each box."

Tracy flipped one over: One hundred and seventy-five dollars. She swallowed hard. Then she turned over another: twenty dollars less. Well, at least she was moving in the right direction. After standing all the boxes on their heads, it appeared the least expensive model was seventy-five dollars, much more than she had really planned on spending for a Secret Santa gift—about ten times the amount, actually.

*Oh well.* Her shoulders sagged in disappointment. She remembered how Donna had gone on and on once about an old music box her grandmother had left her and how heartbroken she had been when it broke.

The clerk, sensing the sale slipping through his bony fingers, spoke in a stage whisper. "I can let you have ten dollars off one of the smaller boxes."

Tracy hesitated, then pointed to one carved from solid cherry, with a maple lid. The design was intriguingly simple, yet gorgeous—a flower, in the first stage of bloom. She looked at the list of songs and chose—what else—"The Rose." She handed over her credit card with a sigh, but knew it would be worth it in the long run just to see Donna's face when she unwrapped the gift.

*This'll make her sorry she dumped me...* And, after all, wasn't that the whole point? Tracy felt her mood lighten as if someone had removed all eight reindeer from her back.

Now all she had to do was to keep the present out of sight for two weeks so Marie wouldn't freak out. How hard could that be?

"I had an accident." Marie spoke matter-of-factly.

"What?" Tracy pressed the headset closer to her ear, not sure she'd heard right.

"An accident."

"Are you okay? What kind of accident?" Tracy's heart pounded as she imagined broken limbs, scars or a missing pinky.

"I *accidentally* found the Christmas present you bought me. Oh, Trace—I absolutely love it!"

*Uh oh...*

"Marie—"

"I'm sorry I snooped, but you know me. And you really didn't hide it very well."

"Marie—"

"I love it, love it, love it! It's beautiful. The flower, just starting to open—like our relationship. I didn't know you were so romantic. And the song—it's one of my all time favorites! You're the best girlfriend I ever had!"

"Damn it, Marie, stop talking for a minute and listen!"

"What's wrong? You're not mad at me, are you?"

"It's not for you." There, she'd said it.

"What? Of course it is. Who else would it be for? Nice try, Trace, but it won't work. I'm sorry I wrecked your surprise. I promise I'll make it up to you . . ." Marie cooed, suggestively.

"No, really. It's not for you."

"Okay. Whatever you say." Marie's voice was patronizing.

Tracy scrambled for a good explanation—anything but the truth. "Marie, I swear—it's for—my mother."

"Your mother, right. That's a good one," Marie laughed.

"It is."

"You haven't spoken to your mother in over a year."

"Yeah, well—that's why. It's a . . . a peace offering. My brother called the other day and said—um . . . she hasn't been feeling all that well, and, uh . . . I wouldn't want anything to happen before we, you know, ironed out our differences."

"Uh huh." Marie was still skeptical, but her confidence was fading fast.

94

"Really. I'm sorry if you're disappointed." Tracy tried her best to sound earnest.

"Well, then . . ." Marie's voice was at least ten degrees cooler. "I really feel like an ass, now."

"No, don't."

"I do. I'm so embarrassed."

"Marie—"

"You must think I'm a jerk."

"No, I—"

"I didn't *think* you'd get me something so expensive, but then I saw it in the closet and I just *assumed*—"

"Marie—"

"I shouldn't have been so nosy. I wouldn't blame you if you just put a big, fat lump of coal in my stocking. That's what I deserve. What an ass . . ." And then, "Can I be there when you make up with your mom? When are you going?"

Tracy panicked. *So much for that idea . . .* "Oh, it's for you."

"What? Really?"

"Yeah."

Marie squealed with delight. "Oh my God! I knew it! You witch! You really had me going. What a *great* present! I feel bad—all I got you was a couple of CDs. But it's the thought that counts, right? Can I have it now? I mean, you're not going to bother wrapping it, are you? That would be crazy since I already know what it is. So, can I have it?"

Tracy surrendered. "Sure."

"Thank you so much. It's the best Christmas present any-one's ever given me."

"Okay. I gotta go, Marie. Gina's giving me the evil eye."

"Oh, right. Sorry to call you at work. I'm making you some-thing really special for dinner tonight. And then we'll talk about dessert . . ." Marie's voice dripped with seductive promise.

"Sounds good. See you later." Tracy hung up.

*Back to square one . . .* And the office party was tomorrow.

"Okay, people—half an hour, then back to the phones," Gina proclaimed, waving her hand like the Queen, then disappearing into her office, too important to mix with the peasants.

Everyone dove for the brownies and punch, hoping but doubting either was spiked.

Tracy used a key to break through the shrink-wrap on her gift so she could read the CD booklet. An image registered from the corner of her eye and her shoulders tensed instinctively as Donna approached.

"Thanks for the book." Donna smiled, shyly.

Tracy shrugged, trying not to stare at her ex-girlfriend's nicely filled-out sweater. "Sure."

"I feel kind of stupid."

"Why? It's just a book."

It was strange, speaking after not speaking for so long. Tracy was surprised to realize how fast her heart was beating.

"I have a confession." Donna looked sheepish.

"Wait, I'll go find a priest," Tracy joked, nervously.

"I picked your name out of the can, but I traded with Jody."

Tracy laughed so hard, she spilled her drink.

"You think that's funny?"

Tracy caught her breath. "It's a long story."

"Okay. Well, anyway . . . I'm sorry I did that. It was dumb."

"It doesn't matter."

"Well, anyway . . . Merry Christmas, I guess."

Tracy watched Donna disappear back into the crowd of co-workers. How easily she blended in. Just another face. Just another sweater. Just another memory—both bitter and sweet. She was suddenly glad she hadn't given Donna the music box after all. It wouldn't have been for the right reason.

Tracy felt an unexpected rush of warmth. She wondered if maybe someone really had spiked the punch. She listened as the others burst into an impromptu medley of Christmas carols. For a moment, she felt alone; then she crossed the room and joined the party, singing along at the top of her lungs.

# TINY DANCER

# Holly Farris

"Reet, I wish you wouldn't. Does it have to be today?" I bargained into the shoulder of her denim jacket. She had already stepped through the doorway onto our front stoop.

Sylvia's truck lurked across the street, a shiny vulture ready to enfold my departing love. Years longer than the time we struggled as a couple Marguerite had already pledged to Sylvia—or at least the next two or three camping trips.

It had been over between us since Thanksgiving; she left on Christmas Eve 1999. Traumatic Turkey Day 1997, the day she admitted sleeping with Sylvia, was long past, the hurt a toothache that got better so gradually it was impossible to tell when the pain stopped. It all came down to arithmetic, Reet had explained: Sylvia was half her age, had four times my stamina (in pursuits more enchanting than carrying a fifty-pound backpack).

Most everything between us was resolved. We, more than her new lover, broke us up, so we plotted arrangements, guilt equally apportioned. I bought the house from her, she planted her Christmas gift azalea from me that year over at Sylvia's, and we lived as housemates for two years beyond.

"Because . . . because he comes today," I reasoned, my last try. Shifting the neon-zippered bag into her left hand, Reet tugged my gray braid forward, into the hollow between collarbone and neck.

"Love to meet him, Eva," she said, stepping off my stoop, possessiveness that stung when I thought it. Sylvia tooted and they both waved from rolled-down windows when they got turned around to drive away.

What a mess—the living room, not my life.

Edgy about just this departure, I'd taken boxes and boxes of Christmas ornaments from our double—now half-empty—closet, all of which lay stacked, unopened, on the dusty wideboard floor. Two chipped blue latte cups sat dirty, twins on the dresser, perhaps for the last time.

For years these dishes tied us. This day, newspaper-wrapped, nestled in Hammermill boxes, all of Marguerite's dishes except the two cups were packed for Sylvia's next drive by. Crockery connected us. Blue milky bowl in the sink—Reet has a busy day at work. Small chipped blue salad plate left on the counter—Eva eats salad before her poetry group meets.

Rinsing her cup, seeing froth dried in a small heart shape, the last place her lips had touched, I put that one in the dishwasher for Hal. Mine I left smudged in the sink.

Richard Thompson complained bitterly through several songs about fickle girlfriends while I danced, dusting golden floorboards with sock feet. Exuberant that it was nearly noon on the day to pick him up, I didn't notice the box until I stubbed a toe against it. It lay beneath the spindly, untrustworthy Christmas tree stand, a red and green insect of a gadget that wouldn't support a handkerchief.

Tiny Dancer, the box advertised to anyone who'd look, black letters indented in the thick pasteboard lid. As if the name were not enough to attract the curious, gold leaf shone on the outside edges of each letter. It was 1950's calligraphy at its height.

I hated it.

Not the box. I liked the box Christmas morning, 1960.

My younger brother and I had been shredding wrapping paper since dawn, dressed in sizes four and eight Roy Rogers pajamas with rubber feet. We'd played gunslingers awhile with our new holsters sagging from small waists and the metal toy pistols, also identical, that were our favorite gifts.

My new fake-leather doctor's bag containing a sinister hypodermic needle on a graduated plastic syringe was next. Timmy opened wide so I could probe with the dry tongue depressor stick, the first part of the charade to end, predictably, with a diagnosis of strep throat, big shot of penicillin to follow.

When I turned around, Dad was behind me, Tiny Dancer in his arms. Holding the box toward me like some fragile fabric draping and trailing onto his corduroy bedroom slippers, he waited. Timmy, mouth closed, shined his pistol. Mom, surveying from the couch, took a jerky, short sip of coffee.

I could not imagine what was inside. Squeaking a little, as I had when my greedy paws found the other treasures, I took the box from his outstretched arms, surprised at how light it was. I set it carefully between my non-skid feet, separated in good gunslinger stance in case I needed to pivot and fire at Tim.

"Because you're older," Dad said.

I could feel his smile warming my back like sunshine when I knelt to look inside. Lid flipped off the unwrapped box, tissue paper clouds threatened to float right out of the container. He'd given Mom nighties most years with less fluff than this.

I actually used the tongue depressor to unfold white filmy sheets.

Hair was the first thing I saw.

Tiny Dancer was a ballerina, something even an eight-year-old should have guessed. I unwrapped her, head to pointed toe, and her features shocked me.

White-blonde hair which, I learned later, was a human hair wig, as soft and fragile as corn silk curled. Tiny red barrettes and spidery silver clips were buried above her forehead and over each tiny shell-pink ear, holding the wisps in place.

Stage make-up adorned her heart-shaped face. Red lipstick traced a perfect mouth centered below rouged cheeks. Flawless straight nose, nostrils painted dots on molded plastic dents. Eyelashes, also curled and stiffened, were ash-blonde human hair. Cheek dimples were perpetual.

In her throat hollow rested a miniature cameo attached to a fine gold chain. Her silk shirt was open, pearl buttons undone, and breasts curved toward one another, pink cleavage aglow.

Out of short, black exercise pants jutted the most phenomenal legs any girl-kid or woman could imagine. Muscles fairly rippled underneath tight pink skin, curves so gradual they had to be felt under my stubby finger to be believed. Practice toe-shoes padded small feet below her graceful ankles, but showcased arches nearly architectural. Years later, I can't say I was surprised when I finally untied the white narrow ribbon cinching the shoes and found ten polished nails.

I strangled on drool and used the fake-coughing fit to collect my thoughts. From the way Mom and Dad beamed from the orange couch, I knew I had to appear pleased. Timmy fired off a few point-blank shots at TD's torso.

I grinned, as hugely as I had at the doctor bag. "Uh, thanks!" I gushed. And tried to replace the lettered lid.

"The best part," Dad directed, blowing cigarette smoke toward tissue paper clouds still inside. "Keep going."

Tutu, long gown with side slits, two more pairs of be-ribboned pointy shoes were what I found, each more outrageous and/or sequined than the last. Scraping the bottom of the box, my small palms mashed the familiar: stick and string.

"Huh?" I asked, thrilled to be back in my element.

"Oh, Eva," Mom trilled.

Dad stubbed out the cigarette, stepping over to help. "See, hon, she's a marionette! A string puppet, it's called marionette. She can be almost alive."

With that, as if rigging the finest model ship his own ten-year-old heart lusted after, he tied and twisted all eight separate and confusing threads onto the wooden T-shaped stick. Then found miniature eye-screws on shoulders, hips and appendages of the lovely miss. Everything assembled, he jostled her up and down in front of our family.

"Yeah," I said when I reached out a finger to pluck the first string.

"You'll learn how, Eva," Dad said, about my lack of coordination when he untangled knots toward evening. "Let's set her on your dresser, out of Tim's reach."

That Christmas night 1960 was the first torture Tiny Dancer had inflicted, though hardly the last.

We'd been in pajamas all day, allowed to eat turkey and gravy in cowboy garb, so it was easy for Dad to slide Timmy into bed around seven. Older sister, I stayed awake until eight.

Thanking them again for the gifts, thinking of the new baby doll Amelia I could strip and set up in her hospital bed tomorrow, I yawned my way upstairs. Merry Christmas and Happy

Trails, they'd said. I was asleep before I replayed opening the holster.

When I awoke with a start, I believed someone was in my room. Grateful for the lariat nightlight, I could see the closet door closed, last year's dolls in the pneumonia ward, some with tiny thermometers poking straight out from the round hole their designers intended for plastic bottle nipples. All was in order.

I relaxed enough to look at the blank ceiling, to search for the crack heavy eyes could trace to send me back to dreamland.

Tarantula!

A frizzed knot, legs and hair, nearly made me scream. Still as I was, it stalked slowly, turning this way and that. Much as I'd dreaded nighttime over years of childhood, I wondered why tonight the fearsome scene played out on the white screen above. Until I saw a pinpoint of light moving across the creature.

The marionette collapsed upon my dresser had created the illusion. Branches moved outside, casting shadows. Intense moonlight mirrored off the White Christmas snowfall we'd had, magnifying the lady's strings. A sequin, reflected, pierced the blackness.

When my first love in seventh grade saw Tiny Dancer, she was unimpressed. "A grown-up lady," she said. Her thumb pressed the flesh between the pink plastic breasts, reminding me how I feared getting older, more ladylike, on that Christmas. To reassure myself that night, I'd found my own nipples, as flat and small as pennies beneath the printed pajama top.

"Let's take off her pants. See if she has hair like my mother," my mature friend said.

I swooned to have a beloved in my room long enough for her to unveil, literally, the facts. Not that I knew the answer, because exercise pants were all the ballerina wore, appropriate to my fumbling with her strings, depriving her of innate grace.

Although I changed her slippers, the shimmery gown—slit to the waist—disgusted me, even in a heap. Once she got very sick after I made her buck and jive, for which a big shot in her silk butt was curative. To spare myself seeing her overnight, I began covering her on my dresser, about the time Dad switched from my cheek to kissing the top of my head, a hurried kitchen good morning. Fitting for a growing-up daughter.

When a sophomore in high school, I did the only physical damage the marionette suffered. Practicing how I'd kiss Laura if she'd ever stop throwing stinging softballs to me on the dusty field, I bit the dancer's central lipstick off. Then, to learn patience, practice forbearance (if not foreplay), I fondled her shapely calves gently, retied her leather-bottom shoes.

At college, I lived years without her. In fact, Mom packed up my room, offered the space to guests in my absence. "We have a guest room," she crowed to far-flung family, as proudly as if they'd put in a pool. Girlfriends and I were not invited to sleep together under the repainted ceiling, though I hinted, pining for an invitation.

Enduring shabby apartment closets and crowded house attics, indignities mounted, but she traveled with me, cramped inside her cardboard home for decades. In one of the early years Reet and I had a tree, I displayed boxes of ornaments I'd picked up at Mom's the first Thanksgiving my mother was a widow.

"I don't know," I backtracked, before I lifted off the lid.

"She's . . . beautiful," Reet said, "very fragile, perfect. If she's important to you . . ." She gestured toward our bedraggled pine trunk.

"I was afraid of her. Never could work those strings."

"She can just sit. Underneath the tree. She's us when we grow up." Tiny watched us make love on the floor.

"Not this year," I said to Hal as soon as I held him.

Overjoyed we could finally be together, he peed down the front of my flannel shirt, kicked his baby legs to jump down. The brindle Scottie puppy was perfect, exactly as he looked in the photos the breeder sent us. Me and Reet, when we decided to adopt him.

I drove us through empty streets in the warehouse district of town, testing the little dog for stamina against car sickness. From the back of my wagon, I heard gurgling followed by a polite cough. Sure thing, Hal'd puked, I saw when I opened the hatch.

Wiping his bristly beard with my plaid forearm, I reached under his doughy belly, stopping his wagging tail mid-thump. Set onto the gravel lot, he pulled the thin tartan leash in the direction of the first tree he saw, a scrub white pine.

We were in a Christmas tree lot, a stop that cost me six dollars when he performed his first precious leg-lift, dousing needles on the closest forlorn branch. Intimately relieved, snoring when I stowed him next to the so-called tree in the back, he forgave my first lie.

"Guess we will this year after all," I said as I landed him and the branch simultaneously on the living room floor, one novelty in each arm. Puppy slurps from Reet's cup filled to the rim with fresh water was a reminder that I'd need to walk him again before long. He danced off on silver toes, snooting the corners where dust bunnies caught in his black beard.

Keeping an eye on him, I set up our tree, using two fingers on one hand, an accomplishment that sent me to the closet for surplus decorations. Hal's leftover water filled the shallow holder; a pillowcase draped just so was sufficient tree skirt.

Tiny was last to move into wonderland. In honor of the occasion, I stripped her, replacing exercise wear with perform-ance attire. Looping spaghetti straps over her thin arms, I stretched leotard fabric across ample breasts, smoothing it into her crotch. Tutu took me more than one try to button, but I managed the pearl dots. Stiff tulle skirt stuck straight out. Pushing her into a sit on the tree skirt, I crossed her long legs, cupping manicured hands. After I tied her shoes and raked her tousled hair, she was a vision at the base of the still-naked tree.

Lights! One strand would do for the diameter involved. Macho Hal, crouched in a girl-puppy squat, had already dampened the bathroom rug, so walking him again would be time wasted. As before, he crumpled into dreams, this time resting his squarish muzzle on a fleece red and gold star, the toy I propped near his cup. I could dash, be back before he noticed.

Wrangling with a clerk who'd rather have been at home, deciding flashing red or white non-chasing, the jaunt took me an hour total.

In the end, Reet decided. She had favored blue ornaments and white lights, the collection she moved to Sylvia's, because it reminded her of moonlight on snow. Unimaginatively, I continued the tradition for me and Hal, daydreaming about the snowfalls we'd share.

Not that I expected one immediately.

That was my first impression as I stepped into the kitchen from the carport. The water cup rested on its side like a fat bug unable to gain traction. Wet paw prints traced the puppy's route toward the living room, into the drift. White—and yellow plus blue and red and silver—lay in mounds. A flake or two floated before landing, mixing with dust, on the wood floor. Hal, wagging furiously, face and front paws grizzled with the mixture, smiled crookedly.

Every molecule of Tiny Dancer was separated from its neighbor. Metal and plastic, hair and chin, net and silk, thigh and finger I inventoried at first glance. White shreds and strings were contributed by the pillowcase, also eaten. Such a feast he'd enjoyed, though nothing significant was swallowed, a fact the grouchy vet confirmed in emergency clinic.

Driving home, I couldn't stop laughing. For the second time on Christmas Eve, he puked in my car, but came home refreshed, restored. As did I. Feeling much better, that is.

Sweeping the fragments into the dustpan, rejoicing that she wouldn't haunt me, I knelt in front of the unadorned pine to scratch a red barrette out of Hal's ear fuzz. When Richard Thompson sang his plans for the next girl he'd find, I joined in on the words I knew.

# An Old-Fashioned Girl

# Rita Stumps

I had just sat down to my Sunday morning paper and a good cup of coffee when the phone rang. Now *who*, I asked myself, just *who* would have the nerve to disturb me at ten on a Sunday morning, the only time each week when I had a chance to relax? The only day not filled with work, laundry, or other household chores. I picked up the receiver.

A female voice asked, "Have I reached 555-1219?"

"Who are you trying to reach?"

"I'm a little embarrassed to say . . . are you by any chance 'an old-fashioned girl'?"

"Oh my God. I can't believe . . . oh, man . . . are you referring to the ad in the *Lesbian Monthly*?"

Finally a response. My personal ad had run two months previously: "Old-fashioned girl, feminine but no makeup, seeks a warm, caring butch for friendship, dating, maybe marriage. Non-drinker, non-smoker, no drugs, please. No game-playing. I'm the kind of girl you'd take home to Mama. 555-1219." So far no one had called, except for the few prank callers who got a kick out of sexual harassment, not really believing that someone like me existed.

I really am an old-fashioned girl, and I had grown tired of the one-night stands, the games, the drinking and drugs. Those things had never been me, but I seemed to have an incredibly hard time finding someone else who felt as I did. When I placed the ad, I had decided to be honest. My reward had been . . . well, I wasn't any worse off—I had been alone before, and I remained alone. And now this caller. Inwardly, I sighed, expecting the worst.

"Yes! Exactly! Well, are you still looking?" Her voice was enthusiastic. "I mean, I know the ad appeared quite a while ago . . . have you found anyone yet?"

"Not exactly." I was hesitant. Was this a joke, or was the caller for real? "How can I help you?"

"My, you certainly do sound old-fashioned. Did you really mean that—'the kind of girl you'd take home to Mama'?"

"Look. Let me be honest. Yes, I'm nice and sweet, or at least that's what my friends always tell me, and I don't want anyone else to take advantage of me. That's all. If this is a crank call, please hang up, or I'll do it first."

"No, don't hang up! I'm real! Honestly! It's just that . . . well, I have a bit of a dilemma, and I wondered if you could help."

"What do you mean? Do you want a date or not?"

"Well, yes and no. You see, I'm supposed to go to my parents' house for Thanksgiving this coming Thursday. My two older brothers always bring their families . . . they both have these really nice wives, and kids, and all . . . I was wondering, would you be my date? For Thanksgiving with my family?"

"Say *what*? I don't think I understand."

"Look, I can even pay you. Just go with me to my parents' for Thanksgiving, pretend you're my long-time girlfriend, and be yourself—sweet and nice. I just want my parents to think I have someone, so they'll stop bugging me about meeting the right man and settling down."

"Don't they know you're a lesbian? Are you out to them?"

"Well, yes, I'm out to them, but I can't seem to find the right relationship, so they don't really believe me. They think the right man will still come along and sweep me off my feet."

"I'm sorry, but this whole thing seems rather strange to me—"

"How about I give you my number? You can call right back, so you'll know this is a genuine call—"

"You really mean it, don't you? About Thanksgiving and everything?"

"Yes . . . oh, no. It just occurred to me. You're probably not even available. You must be going somewhere already."

"It just happens my family lives in North Carolina. No, I don't have plans so far."

"Then you'll do it? Please?"

"On one condition. I will meet you there. And no way will you pay me anything. I guess I mean under two conditions."

"We can't arrive in separate cars. Can we meet somewhere, and you ride with me?"

As we continued to negotiate, my mind kept telling me to back out. My heart was beating wildly, and my face was getting sweaty. What the hell was I getting myself into?

She sounded really happy. "Oh, yeah, old-fashioned girl, what's your real name?"

"My name?" I laughed. "Johanna, but everyone calls me Hanna. Hanna Lehmann."

"I'm Ellie. Short for Ellen. Ellen Herbst."

"Great, Ellen Herbst. By the way, I'm about five foot one, short red hair, big brown eyes, slight build. I'll be wearing a dark green dress, no makeup."

"And I'm five-four, thick, brown, wavy hair, long in back, short in front, typical dyke-do. Medium build, not heavy, not thin. I'll be wearing dark blue pants and a white button-down shirt."

We exchanged a bit more information, then I returned to my paper and coffee. But the mood was gone. For the rest of the day I kept thinking about that sultry voice on the phone, wondering what its owner was really like, and getting excited about the prospect of meeting her. Like it or not, I was attracted to that voice. My mind had begun exploring the romantic possibilities; I was hooked.

The week passed slowly. I somehow made it to the library

where I work, sat at the computer doing my job as a database technician, but my thoughts were elsewhere. I suppose I should have considered the logistics of my upcoming adventure—how *does* a person convince the family of a complete stranger that she's been dating their daughter for a while? But my mind doesn't work that way. I kept thinking about that voice, and imagining the person behind it. I played with the sound of her name on my tongue, as we shared mental conversations—*Ellie*, I would say, *Ellie darling* or, *Ell, honey* . . . maybe sometimes, in serious conversation, *Ellen*. I imagined candlelight at a romantic dinner, or at a quiet evening at home, *our* home. Silly girl, I would remind myself, you haven't even met her yet.

In spite of it all, the week passed. There *are* just three days between Sunday and Thursday, after all. On the big day I woke up with my stomach in knots. Damn it all. I should have told her the burgundy dress; it really is more flattering. Several times I reached for the phone, only to stop and remind myself, You'll be fine. The green dress is wonderful. Besides, what if she turns out to be a complete loser? No need to waste your best dress on a loser.

The minutes passed like hours, but noon came, and there I was, driving my car in the San Fernando Valley's Studio City. I parked on the side street bordering the parking lot where we had agreed to meet, and carefully looked around.

I spotted her immediately, standing near the front doors of the market, not too far from me. She was absolutely gorgeous, with lush, dark brown hair just as she had described it, short in front, long in back. She had, however, neglected to mention the beautiful, generous smile on her face, the dimple in her right cheek, and the amazing, deep, sparkling brown-bordering-on-olive eyes. My palms broke out in a sweat.

She stood there, casually shifting her weight from one foot to the other. She held a beautiful corsage; brilliant flowers bloomed in the brightest of fall colors—deep reds, burning oranges, bright yellows.

Taking a deep breath, I got out of my car.

Ellie's smile grew even bigger as I approached. She looked me up and down appreciatively, nodding in approval. I could see her chest rise as she took in a deep breath; she then looked me in the eyes.

"Hi," she said. "You must be Hanna." She extended a hand, which I shook, and then the other, which held the corsage. "This is for you. I hope you like it."

"Hi, Ellie," I answered. "The flowers are gorgeous. You really didn't need to do that." To my surprise, my voice didn't shake as I spoke. I sounded surprisingly calm in spite of my inner turmoil.

"Here, let me pin it on you," she offered, leaning forward carefully, and gently pinning the flowers onto my dress, just below my left shoulder. I could feel myself blushing as her fingers guided the pin through the green fabric. "My brothers always give their wives flowers. I just felt ... Wait a minute, that didn't come out right ... I mean, you're beautiful, you deserve beautiful things. I'm sorry. There I go, saying the wrong thing again. I just don't know when to shut up sometimes."

I laughed nervously. "That's all right. I'm good at it, too. I mean, talking too much." I inhaled deeply, let the breath back out. "I'm a little nervous." Oh, no, I thought. Now you've done it.

"Really? You look so calm. I'm nervous, too. You're even better than I expected. My parents are going to love you."

I could see her hesitate, as though she wanted to say more. Instead, she gently placed her hand on my elbow, guiding me toward her car.

"I don't mean to rush you, but maybe we ought to get going. Everyone's probably waiting already."

The reality of our situation dawned on me. "How are we going to pull this off?" I asked as we settled into her car. "I don't even know you, and I'm supposed to be your girlfriend?"

"I know, I know." She spoke quietly, in that bedroom-husky voice I remembered from the phone call. "Here's the deal. You tell me everything about yourself, and I'll tell you about me. Everyone in my family likes to talk, so you probably won't get a word in, so if we both have the basics down we should be just fine."

"Still sounds crazy to me, but I'm game." Besides, I really like you, I wanted to say. I wished we were going out on a real date, just the two of us. I wanted more. I wanted *her*, all to myself, alone, romantically. I barely stopped myself from leaning over and kissing her. I finally managed to speak. "So tell me about yourself," I said.

"I'm an assistant manager at Pets Unlimited in Encino. I'm thirty-five years old—my birthday is December sixteenth."

"I *love* Pets Unlimited! I shop at the North Hollywood location! My cats adore that catnip you sell . . . they just can't get enough of it. And everyone at the store is so friendly! What a cool place to work!"

Ellie laughed, a wonderful, genuine, vibrant sound. She laughed with her whole body, throwing her head back, arching her body slightly. "You've been going to the wrong location. Come to my store sometime. We're even better than North Hollywood.

"We're almost there," she warned. "You'd better tell me about yourself, quickly."

"Oh, yeah . . . Library Assistant, database technician. I sit at a computer all day, editing information in our library's computer. I'm thirty, a Capricorn, born on January first."

"You're kidding. A New Year's baby?"

"Yes. Most of the time people are too hung over to remember. I can't really blame them—I love New Year's Eve."

"Me, too. I just don't like drinking. Just like in your ad—no drinking, no smoking, no drugs. I feel like we're soul mates already." She suddenly got quiet, as though she'd said too much. "I'm sorry . . . I didn't mean to be so forward."

I touched her arm lightly. "I feel the same way," I murmured.

"Really?"

"Yeah."

We spoke little for the rest of the drive, both of us absorbing the feeling that there was more between us already. I felt calm, peaceful, comfortable. My hand remained on her arm, something she seemed to like. She reached over once, and lightly brushed the side of my face. I found it hard to concentrate.

By the time we reached her parents' modest home in Van Nuys, it had taken both forever and no time at all. I was nervous and excited; she seemed calm. After she parked the car, we looked at each other. Ellie smiled.

"Here we go," she commented.

"We'll be fine," I replied. I took her hand and squeezed it. She squeezed back, looking down at me. She kept my hand in hers as we walked to the front door of the house.

An elegant, older woman greeted us at the door. "Ellie!" she cried out. "You're here! We've been waiting for you!" She noticed me. "And this must be your friend. I'm sorry, dear, but I've forgotten your name. I'm Fran Herbst. It's so very nice to meet you. Ellie hasn't told us a whole lot about you, but I can already tell—you seem like a very nice young lady."

I didn't quite know what to say. "Nice to meet you, too." Good start. "My name is Hanna Lehmann."

"Hanna, how wonderful you could be with us today. Please come in." Fran tucked one hand through my arm, the other through Ellie's, and whisked us both into the house. Pandemonium broke out. A large group of adults and kids swarmed around us, greetings flying everywhere.

"Ellie!" people shouted, running up to hug her. I got my share of hugs, too, along with lots of "so glad you could be here." The names whirled in and out of my head; I knew only that the oldest man was Ellie's father, the two younger men her brothers, the women her sisters-in-law, and that both couples had plenty of children. I counted six of them. Two dogs also joined in, dashing around everyone. Somewhere in the midst of all the noise Ellie disappeared, along with some of the children. Uh oh, I thought. Now what do I do? I kept smiling and nodding, chatting up a storm, although I don't remember a thing I said. Everything was a blur to me.

Soon, in a manner typical of the few hetero parties I had ever attended, the group naturally divided itself, and the women ended up in the kitchen, doing last-minute food preparation. The men wandered off into the living room, where a football game played on the TV set.

I felt more and more lost. Ellie had not returned. I had never met any of these people before in my life, would probably never see them again, and I had no idea of what to say to them. I guess I did all right, though, because somehow the conversation flowed. Until suddenly the attention turned to me.

"So how long have you and Ellie been together?" asked Fran. "I don't believe she's ever mentioned you before."

I looked around frantically, not knowing how to answer. Fran noticed, and continued, "Oh, don't worry. She's probably off playing Nintendo with the kids. She does love Nintendo, don't you agree?"

"Oh, yes," I stammered. "She sure does. Yes, that must be it. She especially loves basketball."

Fran looked thoughtful, about to say something, then seemed to change her mind. Thankfully, Ellie chose that moment to wander into the kitchen. My mouth slightly open, I turned toward her, my eyes full of questions.

"Sorry, I've been busy with Super Mario," Ellie explained.

I was relieved she had returned. "Ellie—tell your mom how long we've been together!"

A look of panic quickly crossed her face as she stuttered, "Oh, about seven months."

"Yes," I repeated. "About seven months."

Fran looked puzzled.

"But, Ellie, dear, you've never even mentioned Hanna before. And she seems like a lovely person. Why haven't you told us about her?"

This time, Ellie looked to me for help.

"Uh, well, gee, we've been so busy, what with our jobs and everything," I stammered. Damn, I thought. Not very clever, certainly not original. I blew it.

Fran's brows pulled together slightly in a quizzical look, but she drew her attention back to the turkey, which she was retrieving from the oven. "Yes, I keep forgetting. You young people work so hard." As she lifted the turkey onto a platter, she directed her words to Ellie. "You really should have mentioned Hanna sooner. You've been hiding a good thing from your family!"

Ellie and I both blushed. I nervously reached out for some bowls of mashed potatoes and green beans; Ellie busied herself by grabbing a dish of yams. The two sisters-in-law had already gone into the dining room with some other platters; we followed them.

"Dinner's served!" Fran called out as she set the turkey onto the middle of the table. Men and children appeared from nowhere, and everyone settled down to eat.

Fran seemed to have made it her duty to find out more about me, because she immediately began to ask questions.

"So, Hanna, tell me more about yourself. Does your family live nearby?"

"No, they live in North Carolina, so I don't see them that often."

Ellie jumped right in. "But they did call this morning, and wish us a happy Thanksgiving!"

"How nice," remarked Fran. "Marty," she addressed her husband, who sat across from her, "isn't that nice, her family lives in North Carolina. Don't you have some cousins there?"

"Yes, yes," boomed Marty. "They own a toy store. In Charlotte, I think."

"That's where Hanna's parents live! In Charlotte!" Ellie said excitedly. I looked at her, shocked.

"Ellie, don't you remember? My parents don't live in Charlotte; they're in Greensboro."

Ellie turned bright red. "Oh, yeah, that's right." Even her ears blushed. "Sorry, Hanna, I forgot."

Fran's face once again took on a puzzled look. She opened her mouth to speak, but again changed her mind.

"And do you ever visit them?" she finally said, after a few minutes during which she ate silently, deep in thought. Thankfully, no one had noticed. People were all busy with conversations of their own.

"No, not very often. We're not very close."

"Not even for the holidays, for Hanukkah?"

"Hanukkah? Oh my, oh no, I mean, oh no. No, we're not Jewish." Fran appeared startled; Ellie looked downright shocked.

"You're not Jewish?" They both exclaimed at once.

"Well, no, not really."

"But your last name is Lehmann!" This from Ellie.

"Yes, we're from Germany. We moved to the United States when I was seven. I came to L.A. to go to college, and never returned to Greensboro." I felt really embarrassed. What must Ellie think now, I wondered. Her whole family must really hate me. They had every right to, after what happened in World War II.

"Well." Fran took a deep breath, straightening her shoulders. "I'm sorry, I'm just very surprised. You see, I don't think Ellie's ever gone out with anyone who's not Jewish. You're still very nice and sweet. In fact, I think I would say you almost seem a little bit old-fashioned, what with your nice manners and all. Please, welcome to the family. We really enjoy having you here."

I had slowly turned my face downward, so that I was staring at my hands in my lap. As her words registered, I looked back up, stunned.

"You mean, you still like me?" I addressed the question to Fran, but Ellie was the one who responded.

"Even more than ever," she said. She then turned to her mother. "Mom, I have a confession to make . . ."

Her mother's eyes twinkled as she looked over at her daughter. "I know, dear. You really haven't known Hanna for very long, have you?"

"How did you figure it out?" Ellie exclaimed.

"Well, I don't know the details, but you sure didn't seem to know very much about her. Be honest with me—how long have you known each other?"

Ellie eyes caught mine, and we both laughed. We laughed and laughed, until tears streamed down our faces. Others sitting at the table stopped their conversations—obviously, something much more interesting had happened at our end.

"Oh, Mom," she finally gasped. "What do you think, Hanna? How long have we known each other?"

"You mean including the phone conversation? I'd say a total of two hours or so."

At that point, Ellie explained the whole story. Needless to say, everyone at the table was quite intrigued. As Ellie gave the details of our meeting, chuckles occasionally burst out.

"I simply can't believe this," Marty finally said, his wife

having run out of words. "My dear Ellie, may I give you just a bit of advice?"

Ellie looked as if she expected reprimanding. "Yes, Dad?"

"Hold onto her. Any girl who could put up with a stunt like that is a real keeper!"

Applause broke out around the table. Ellie reached for my hand, and gazed into my eyes. "Next time," she said, "how would you like to go out on a real date?"

"I would love it. How about tomorrow night?" I replied, looking right back at her.

"Sounds great." She grinned.

All the rest of the day, we held hands. I kept looking at her, she kept looking at me, and I knew I was falling in love.

Later that evening, when she finally took me home, I knew she was falling in love, too. It was all in the way she kissed me goodnight.

# WINTER SOLSTICE: THE CAT'S MEOW

## Barbara Kahn

CHARACTERS:    JULIE, *a young woman who lives in the building.*
ZENA, *a young woman who doesn't.*

TIME:    *Saturday, December 21, 1996. Late afternoon.*
SCENE:    *An apartment building.*

*There are two apartments separated by a hallway. JULIE is in one, at a kitchen counter, preparing a salad in a wooden bowl. On the floor is an open paper bag from A&P or Sloan's. There is a couch in the apartment. JULIE is following a recipe in a small book—*The Supermarket Sorceress. *ZENA is alone in the other apartment, trying to look under and behind the couch.*

JULIE *(adding some ingredients to her salad, she reads from recipe in book).* "This salad is consumed to make yourself more attractive, to invoke beauty, or to bewitch someone."

ZENA *(pleading).* Please, Chloe, please come out. What am I supposed to tell Linda when she calls? "Chloe's probably fine, but I haven't seen her in the week since you've been gone—she's being a little shy with me." *(silence)*

JULIE *(checks the bowl).* Lettuce, asparagus, tomatoes, snow peas ... *(reads)* "Tomatoes and snow peas are sacred to voluptuous Venus." All right! I am tired of being tongue-tied.

ZENA. Okay. Don't show yourself. But do something!

JULIE. All's fair in love and that other thing ...

ZENA *(shaking a box of dry cat food).* You'd show yourself to that woman who lives across the hall. I've seen *her* twice this week, which is two times more than I can say for you. I'll bet you wish Linda had asked *her* to take care of you.

JULIE *(checking bowl again, adding more ingredients, reading from book).* "Hearts of palm"—I already rubbed the bowl with garlic—"pitted black olives, radishes ... Red radishes create lust ..." Yeah! And, finally, "Sprinkle with rose water ..." *(sprinkles the salad)*

ZENA. I give up. *You* are in control here. You are powerful ... and beautiful and wise. *(silence)* Flattery doesn't work either. Well, that's it then. I'm going. I am. I'll see you tomorrow ... I will, won't I?

(ZENA *exits into hallway, looks at the door opposite.*)

126

JULIE. "If you consume the salad, it will increase your animal
magnetism and drawing power. If eaten by another while
in your presence, it will make you irresistible to them."
*(crosses her fingers)*
> (JULIE *tosses the salad and takes a nibble, just as*
> ZENA *rings the buzzer of her apartment. JULIE is*
> *startled. She goes to door, looks through peephole, sees*
> *who it is, gasps. Shocked at how quickly the spell is*
> *working,* JULIE *opens the door. She is dazzled by*
> ZENA *and afraid at what she may have wrought.)*

JULIE. *(terrified)* What?

ZENA. Your keys.

JULIE. Huh?

ZENA. You left your keys in the door.

JULIE. I did?

ZENA. Yes, you did.

JULIE. Oh.

ZENA. Would you like them back?

JULIE *(nervous)*. Whatever.

ZENA. Are you all right? Did I interrupt something?

JULIE. No. I'm fine. How's Chloe?

ZENA. I haven't seen her in a week. I'm beginning to worry
about her.

JULIE. That's great . . . *('comes to' and catches herself)* Oh . . . I
mean, don't worry. I'm sure she's fine. She's just teasing.
She'll show herself to you when she's ready. She'd be crazy
not to.

ZENA.  Well ... I hope so ...

>  *(There is an awkward silence as they stare at each other.)*

JULIE.  Would you like to come in? I promise not to hide from you.

ZENA.  Okay. *(she enters)*

JULIE *(points to couch)*.  Have a seat.

ZENA *(sits)*.  My name's Zena.

JULIE.  The warrior princess! *(smiles broadly)*

ZENA.  Excuse me?

JULIE *(excited)*.  *Xena the Warrior Princess*. I'm Gabrielle! Just kidding. My name's Julie.

ZENA.  I'm sorry. I don't know what you're talking about.

JULIE.  On television.

ZENA.  I don't watch television. Don't have one.

JULIE.  You don't have a television? That's so cool. I'm addicted. Insomnia.

ZENA.  Tell me about Xena the warrior.

JULIE *(sits next to ZENA)*.  The warrior princess. Well, she started out as a villain on *Hercules*—that's another series—but when they did the spinoff, they gave her a change of heart. It all takes place in some pseudo-ancient Europe. Xena travels around saving villages from roving warlords. Gabrielle is her sidekick, who has a big crush on her ... well, they never say that exactly, but they show it. It's the kind of show most of my les—most of my friends would never admit watching. Not me. I'm hopelessly

128

honest about my taste, which sorta runs the gamut. *(pause)* I actually have been known to watch *Masterpiece Theater*... Really. I'm sorry.

ZENA. For what?

JULIE. Talking so much and forgetting my manners. Can I offer you something?

ZENA. Sure.

JULIE. What?

ZENA. What are you offering?

JULIE. Something to drink?

ZENA. Okay.

JULIE. Great.

> *(Silence.)*

ZENA. So...

JULIE *(realizes her distraction)*. Oh, gees... What would you like? I have juice, diet soda, herbal tea... or beer. How about a Corona?

ZENA. Beer's fine. Sounds good.

JULIE. Great. I'll get it.

> *(JULIE starts to get the beer, notices the salad and turns back to ZENA.)*

JULIE. By the way, I just finished making a salad when you rang the bell. I need to make sure I have the right proportions before I let it set... I mean marinate. Would you try it for me? Do you mind? Just a little taste?

ZENA. Oh, sure.

> *(JULIE goes to counter, notices and hides the book. She*

*takes a forkful of salad, closes her eyes and whispers a silent "please." She brings the sample to* ZENA *who takes it.* ZENA *eats it thoughtfully.)*

JULIE.  Well?

ZENA *(trying to be polite).*  It's different. Not bad.

JULIE.  Would you like to uh, you know, uh, have some more?

ZENA.  I'm not much for salad. You should try it yourself.

JULIE.  I will. I'm just going to try it—just a bite. It'll take a second, and then I'll get your beer.

    *(JULIE goes back to salad, takes a taste.)*

ZENA.  So?

JULIE *(disappointed with the taste).*  You were right.

    *(JULIE looks intently at* ZENA, *trying to notice if there is a change.* ZENA *stares back.)*

ZENA.  So, are you a professional chef or is cooking just a hobby?

JULIE.  Oh, you mean because of the salad? That was, uh, sort of an experiment. I work in a law office. In the proof-reading department. *(trying to impress)* I'm a supervisor. How about you?

ZENA.  English lit. Columbia. I'm one of the lucky ones with tenure.

JULIE.  You're a professor?!

ZENA.  I'm afraid so. Associate, actually.

    *(JULIE stares anxiously at* ZENA.*)*

JULIE.  I can't believe that I told you that I watch some stupid, lowbrow television show, and you're a professor.

ZENA. Well, I have a confession to make.

JULIE. What?

ZENA. Sometimes, when I should be working, I turn on my computer and instead of planning for my classes, I play *Minesweeper*.

JULIE *(looks around in exaggerated attempt at secrecy, she 'confides')*. Well I take the Cosmo love quiz every month . . .

ZENA. Ahhh . . . That's not so bad.

JULIE. Yes it is. I fail it every month.

ZENA *(boasting)*. I have a secret collection of toys from McDonald's Happy Meals.

JULIE. Wow! Um, all right. *(thinking hard)* . . . Uh, I once read a novel by Barbara Cartland.

ZENA. Who?

JULIE. See?

ZENA. Who is that?

JULIE. She's English. And you never heard of her, because she writes tacky romance novels.

ZENA *(conceding)*. Good. That's good.

JULIE. It's getting dark. I'd better turn the light on.

    *(JULIE reaches behind ZENA to turn on table lamp, finds herself nose to nose with ZENA. She quickly pulls back, and ZENA turns the lamp on.)*

ZENA. Did you know today's the Winter Solstice, the shortest day of the year?

JULIE. Or the longest night. *(turns her hand back and forth)* You know—half empty, half full . . .

ZENA. In Roman times, this was the Saturnalia—a holiday for debauchery and fun, although I don't imagine they're mutually exclusive. The English call it St. Lucy's Day. John Donne wrote a poem about it. I have a lot of poems in my head.

JULIE. How does it go?

ZENA. You don't really want me to recite poetry, do you?

JULIE. That would be so great. No one ever did that for me before.

ZENA. Well, everyone is entitled to an occasional first in her life.

JULIE. Okay! Thanks.

ZENA. I'll do my best. *(nervous)* It might help if I had that beer. Or just a glass of water.

JULIE *(embarrassed)*. I'm sorry. I totally forgot. I'll get it right now.

ZENA. No problem.

JULIE *(upset at her social 'lapse')*. You probably think I'm some kind of flake or airhead—

ZENA. No, I don't—

JULIE *(interrupting)*. —And you're right. Sometimes I'm so scattered.

ZENA. You're fine. Really—

JULIE *(interrupting again)*. I'm not. You're the professor, and I'm absent-minded.

ZENA. Associate professor—

JULIE. You can remember entire poems, and I can't even remember what I said two minutes ago.

ZENA.  I may not be able to remember it all.

JULIE.  Whatever you remember will be fine.

ZENA.  So, sit down, and we'll see.

JULIE.  Right.

>(JULIE *sits next to* ZENA *on the couch, positions herself with solemnity and gazes intently at* ZENA.)

JULIE.  Okay. I'm ready.

ZENA *(smiles)*.  Here goes.

>(*As she recites, the attraction between them increases;* ZENA's *recitation becomes more romantic and sensual, causing her to forget most of the poem.*)

ZENA.  The title is "A Nocturnal upon St. Lucy's Day, Being the Shortest Day." It's from his love poems.

>(JULIE'S *eyes widen.* ZENA *recites from memory*)

ZENA *(cont.)*.  "Tis the year's midnight, and it is the day's, Lucy's, who scarce seven hours herself unmasks; The Sun is spent," . . . uh . . . "Dead and interred" . . . It goes on from there, more about death and resurrection, Donne was raised a Catholic, but he converted to Church of England and . . . *(stops herself)* I'm sorry . . . Sometimes I act like a teacher. Force of habit.

JULIE.  It's all right. It's really interesting.

ZENA.  You're being polite. I forgot most of it, anyway.

JULIE.  What you remember is wonderful.

ZENA.  Are you sure?

JULIE.  Please go on.

ZENA.  I know the last part.

*(ZENA puts one arm on back of couch behind JULIE.)*

ZENA *(cont.)*. "You lovers, for whose sake the lesser Sun At this time to the Goat is run, To fetch new lust, and give it you,"...

*(ZENA takes JULIE'S hand.)*

ZENA *(cont.)*. "Let me prepare towards her, and let me call This hour her Vigil, and her Eve, since this Both the year's, and the day's deep midnight is."

*(They are locked in each other's gaze.)*

JULIE. Your students are very lucky.

ZENA. Thanks. Speaking of Catholics—I'm not—but I have another confession to make.

JULIE. What? You hate cats? I won't tell Linda.

ZENA *(laughs)*. No. I love cats. Even Chloe. It's just not mutual.

JULIE. What is it then?

ZENA. You said that you're always honest, you don't hide what you like. May I be honest with you?

JULIE. About what?

ZENA. About you... *(takes a deep breath, exhales)* I'm enjoying myself immensely. I think you're attractive—you have beautiful warm eyes and a wonderful smile... Stop me if I'm embarrassing you or myself, or if you're not a lesbian, or if you are a lesbian and not single... *(waits, but JULIE is silent)* Say something.

JULIE. No...

ZENA *(puzzled)*. No?

JULIE. You said to stop you if I'm any of those things that you said and I'm not, so I don't have to stop you. You can keep right on . . .

    *(ZENA cuts her off with a gentle kiss. They pull away slightly, JULIE kisses her back more passionately.)*

ZENA *(smiles).* I also find you charming and refreshingly open and honest. I want to learn more about you . . . *(notices JULIE's expression)* Am I frightening you?

JULIE. No. I really would like to see you again—

ZENA. Great.

JULIE. —But I have to tell you something. *(looking toward salad)* I'm not as honest as you think I am.

ZENA. Would you hold that thought? I need to go to the FedEx office before they close. But I can come back. We could have dinner. Say around six?

JULIE. I'd like that.

ZENA. You decide where . . .

JULIE. You want me to decide?

ZENA. How about the Waverly Inn on Bank Street? I mean Ye Waverly Inn. Have you eaten there?

JULIE. No.

ZENA. You get two firsts in one day. How about it?

JULIE. Sure. We can come back here for dessert. Celebrate Winter Solstice. And drink to St. Lucy.

ZENA. And Saturnalia.

JULIE. What the hell! And Saturnalia, too.

ZENA. I'll be back here at six.

    *(ZENA kisses JULIE again, puts her coat on and exits*

*into hallway. JULIE, excited, goes to the salad, picks up the book and holds it to herself. In the hallway, ZENA reaches in her coat pocket, takes out another copy of the same book, holds it up in triumph, brings it back down and kisses it.)*

ZENA. It worked! It really worked!

JULIE *(looking up).* The beer! I forgot to give her the beer!
*(LIGHTS start to fade. As lights reach black, there is the sound of a low, long meow of a Siamese cat.)*

## CURTAIN

*Winter Solstice* was commissioned and produced by Miranda Theatre Company, New York City (Valentina Fratti, artistic director) for Holidaze, a festival of one-act plays. It was subsequently produced as part of "Crossings: Where W.11th Meets W.4th St, Greenwich Village," a collection of interrelated one-act plays presented by Theater for the New City, New York City (Crystal Field, executive artistic director).

NOTE: Quotes in the play are from *The Supermarket Sorceress* by Lexa Rosean. St. Martin's Press. New York: 1996. Quoted by permission of the author.

# HANUKKAH AT A BAR

## Lee Lynch

Great patches of clouds like assemblies of white smoke puffs filled the sky. The street was silent, as if cold muffled Soho. Sally the bartender, tall and blonde, stood outside Café Femmes, just beyond the lavender awning, her breath turning to steam. Head back, she watched the clouds drift by, sniffed the frozen, sooty air. Were they snow clouds, or did they just look like soft heaps of the stuff poised, waiting like the whole city for Christmas?

No, thought Sally, as she returned to the warm bar, not the whole city. Not Liz, her lover and partner at Café Femmes. Liz and the other Jews of the city weren't waiting for Christmas, but quietly readying for Hanukkah, which would start Sunday, two days away. She picked up the bar rag she'd left on a table and moved around the smoky-smelling room, wiping down every

137

surface. The lunch crowd was neater than the night crowd, but there were pizza stains, dried beer foam, sticky Coke spills. Gabby, who normally took care of the restaurant business, had left early for a doctor appointment and wouldn't be back until the dinner hour.

Hanukkah. It had never been a big deal before. She scrubbed finger smudges off the plastic window of the electronic game. Liz always said she was proud to be a Jew. In their first years together Sally had never failed to give her a present at least on the first of the eight-day celebration. But Hanukkah reminded Liz of her family and she hadn't encouraged Sally. She'd cried enough, Liz had said, over her stubborn, nearly Orthodox father's edict that she never set foot in his home again. Over what she'd lost by being gay. Eventually they'd marked the holiday only by placing a menorah on the bar.

But last spring, for the first time in the fifteen years since Liz had come out to her parents, Mrs. Marks had called to invite Liz to join them for Passover. Liz. Not Liz and Sally. Liz had refused. Now her mother had tried again, wanting her for Hanukkah. And Liz had been overwrought, sleepless, ever since, poised like the snow clouds, wanting to fall back into her family's arms, but wanting also to be her whole self. She was Sally's lover, she said, not just her father's daughter.

A voice called, "Guess I'll have to help myself."

Sally jumped, knocked out of her worried trance. LilyAnn Lee was so tall she was making a habit of silencing the cowbells with her hand before the door hit them.

"You trying to give me heart failure?" asked Sally, rounding the bar, trailing her fingers on its polished wood.

LilyAnn Lee reached across the bar, set the seltzer hose back and lowered herself to her stool. She was six feet tall, solid-looking, her skin an even, glowing dark brown. She crossed her legs, set her elbows on the bar and leaned seductively toward Sally. Her fingernail polish was a shocking metallic magenta, her dangling earrings flashed in the light. A heady perfume filled Sally's nostrils. She shook her head. It had always amazed her how utterly feminine this big woman could make herself. She remembered being struck by that even the first time she'd seen LilyAnn Lee, a freshman entering during Sally's senior year. She'd been sure LilyAnn was gay until she'd next seen her—on the arm of a male athlete.

"You *know* I don't care for those cowbells ringing so close to my sensitive ear," said LilyAnn Lee.

Sally grinned and suggested, "Stoop."

"*I* do not stoop for any white girl's cowbells. Not LilyAnn Lee, M.B.A." She grinned, too. "How's my old pal Sal?"

"You mean besides the heart attack?"

"Come to think of it, you are kind of pale."

"I *am*?" Sally asked, turning to look in the mirror.

"Compared to *what* is the question."

Sally turned back. "Very funny."

"What do you have in the non-alcoholic line?" asked LilyAnn.

"A Lavender Julie?"

"That sticky-sweet grape thing Gabby thrives on? Not for me."

"The Jefferson Lime Squeeze?"

"Say *what*?"

She wiped the bar top between them, grinning again. This would make up for the paleface routine. "You heard me."

"Don't tell me Jefferson is back in town. And not drinking? Well, my, my, will wonders never cease."

Sally filled her in on their old schoolmate, the woman athlete who'd finally brought LilyAnn Lee out.

"What do you call it? A Jefferson Lime *Squeeze*? I'll bet she likes that name. Let me try one—it must be good if it's keeping Jefferson herself off the sauce." Sally poured lime and white grape juices over crushed ice. "You tell her I'm putting fires out now, not starting them in the girls' dorm?" LilyAnn asked.

She nodded. "And that you finished graduate school before you joined the fire department." Despite her sardonic expression, she could tell LilyAnn still cared what Jefferson thought. Kindly, she conceded, "She was impressed."

"Mmm-uh!" said LilyAnn, sucking in her cheeks as she tasted the tart drink. She didn't have to work again until Monday night, she told Sally, and settled in at the bar for the afternoon. Customers came and went as they talked about their old school days. A little later Julie, who managed a florist shop uptown, made her weekly stop with flowers. Sally and LilyAnn worked together, arranging them in little vases on the tables, indulging in their spring-like scents.

"I'm back!" Gabby announced unnecessarily as she slammed the door against the cowbells. Short, stocky, with graying hair brushed back from her forehead, she rushed to the counter and grabbed an apron. "Hey, Big Lil," she said as she began her preparations.

"That was a long doctor appointment," Sally commented with concern. Gabby was never late.

"I—ah—had to make a stop."

"Did she say you're okay?" They all went to Dr. Sterne, who frequented an uptown bar, but promised she'd visit Café Femmes sometime.

"Yeah," said Gabby brusquely, as if completely, uncharacteristically absorbed in her work.

Her silence worried Sally. She lay down the wet bar rag and crossed to stand next to Gabby, watching as she deftly cut salad vegetables, sharp wooden knife in her square fingers. Her eyes looked red, but then she'd just finished a neat stack of fragrant onions. Gabby was only forty. It couldn't be anything that serious, could it?

"Shit!" Gabby said.

Sally saw the blood spurt to the surface of Gabby's thumb, saw her drop the knife, the endive. Then, holding a towel against her cut, Gabby began to cry. Sally put an arm around her shoulder and patted it awkwardly. Gabby cried on, quietly, lifting the bloody towel two-handed to her face to wipe the tears.

"What's going on here?" LilyAnn asked. Sally shrugged, but

LilyAnn seemed to take it all in at once and in a moment had a strip of clean cloth around Gabby's thumb. She held Gabby tight against her breasts. "You're going to have to tell somebody, Little Gab," she said with a soothing tone Sally imagined her using on survivors of fires. "Do you have to be hospitalized?"

Gabby shook her head against LilyAnn's breasts and managed to say, "I don't know. But I hate it, I hate it. Why do bodies have to wear out?" Then she sobbed more.

"What *is* it?" Sally urged. "You know we're family. Have you told Amaretto?"

Gabby nodded. "I stopped there after the tests."

"Tests?" asked Sally and LilyAnn simultaneously.

"It's arrhythmia. It means irregular hearbeat. It could be nothing. But I could die!"

"Oh-ho," Sally joked. "The junk food years are over."

But she felt a coldness around her own heart. Not Gabby. She was finally very, very sober, had a job that suited her, and was with a fine lover.

"Doc Sterne sent me down for more tests today. I see her Monday for the results."

Sally left LilyAnn to minister to Gabby and served a customer at the bar.

She could see through the plate glass window, beyond the backwards words, "CAFÉ FEMMES," that dusk had come.

She moved to the door and stepped outside.

There was an icy chill to the air that made her flesh feel raw.

A lone truck was unloading at the warehouse across the street, its exhaust inescapable. She coughed. With a clang, someone rolled shut the metal door on a loading dock. The city had a feeling of impermanence to it. Cities, bodies, did wear out. Even the little tree newly planted in front of Café Femmes struggled to live. She looked up and saw those smoke-puff clouds still hanging, still full, waiting and waiting for what?

She sighed, tired, and went back in. She'd lost sleep too, with Liz not sleeping. Should she tell Liz about Gabby, or did she have enough on her mind?

But just then Liz arrived, cheeks red from the cold, a soft, pale green scarf wrapped around her neck. She moved as quickly as ever, a woman who meant business, but Sally could see the tension in her limbs, the tautness of her facial muscles, the darkness under her eyes. They entered the bar together. She unwound the scarf from Liz's neck wtih great tenderness. Liz brought the smell of home with her.

"How's it going?" she asked.

"My mother called again." Liz's voice was hoarse. She must have been crying too. Sometimes, Sally thought as she drew a pitcher of cold beer and smiled automatically at the woman who'd ordered, sometimes it seemed as if the whole world was a cloud, filled with moisture and everyone must take a turn in overflowing. She returned to Liz's side. "I asked her if I could bring you. My mate. My companion. My chosen family."

Sally could tell. "She said no."

"She said my father had come a long way. That I should

compromise too. That I was wrong to want the whole schmear at once."

"And you said—"

Liz became agitated. She was polishing her glasses ferociously. "'All at once?' I said to her. 'You're not going to be around forever, Ma. I want my family all at once, yes, and now. All at once,'" she repeated with sarcasm. "After fifteen years of not seeing the inside of my family home."

The Marks family owned a brownstone in Brooklyn and Liz sometimes remembered it aloud, room by room, when she came home in the early morning and climbed in beside the already sleeping Sally, who'd wrap her long legs around Liz and hold her, breathing that home scent, half-dreaming, half-listening, until Liz's brownstone became part of her own dreams, as if she'd grown up there, too.

"You're not going."

"I asked for another day to talk to you about it."

"Right down to the wire."

"I need to know how you feel, Sal. What it would mean to you not to be there."

"Hey, I've lived without Hanukkah for forty-one years now."

"Not good enough, babe. I don't want one of your unfeeling WASP answers."

Sally shrugged, and went to serve a group of office workers on their way home from work. What could she do? She'd been brought up to think of emotions as the equivalent of something you did in the bathroom. Sure she had them, but to lay them down on the bar, or even think about them much, wasn't something she was good at. Sometimes, to tell the truth, Liz carried on a little too much. There she was now, hugging Gabby to death, holding her hand, making much of what might be nothing. She'd have Gabby crying into her endives and sunchokes all night.

She started to leave as soon as Liz was ready to begin her shift. Didn't even kiss her goodbye.

"Are you mad?" Liz asked, catching up with her at the door.

"Mad?" asked Sally, surprised. Now Liz was making another crisis. The office workers were singing "Happy Birthday" noisily and she had to talk over them. "Why should I be mad?"

"Don't shout at me!" Liz said, turning away with tears in her eyes.

Sally stood tall, unbending, and plunged into the chilled air. A web of emotions covered Café Femmes tonight—fear and conflict, longing and self-pity extending into every corner. She was glad to leave it behind. And sorry. She decided to stay in the dark, hushed neighborhood.

"Wait up, girl!" she heard behind her.

It was LilyAnn Lee loping toward her.

"Which way you heading?"

Sally shrugged again. "Just away."

"Walk with me to the fire house. I have to pick up my laundry."

LilyAnn had discovered Café Femmes when she was assigned to the local station. They walked there in silence now, bundled into themselves against the cold, the six-foot black woman, her Afro trimmed down for safety at work, and the tall blonde who could tell her ears were reddening in the stinging wind.

The rest of the company was out on a fire. Sally looked around the drab firehouse and wondered what LilyAnn's life could be like, among all these men.

"Pretty lonely," LilyAnn said later, over a red sauce smelling powerfully of oregano at Sally's favorite candlelit restaurant in Little Italy. They'd stopped at the service laundry around the corner first. "Some of them hate me. Some of them want to get in my pants. In between are one or two who respect me for what I am, who've watched me work and know I'm there for them on a fire, because that's my job, keeping lives going the best way I can."

"My job is cushy compared to that."

"You shitting me? Remember, I worked out there in that business world before I got this job. It's as dangerous as fire-fighting. You just get burnt in different ways. I wouldn't want to work six days a week, every week of the year, put up with organized crime threats and every other racket there is. Look at the risks you take with your money, your security, sitting ducks for queer-bashers. I wouldn't want to listen to the gay kids' problems. Watch the love and the loss, the happiness that's here one day, gone the next. The waste. So many of those kids don't know how lucky they are to have life. They're drinking, drugging it away like it's some miserable sentence they have to get through. No, I'd rather go out on a fire where I know what

146

to expect, what to do when I get there, watch people appreciate life."

"Is that why you went with the fire department? To save lives?"

LilyAnn's eyes sparked like Liz's did when she talked about the old brownstone. "You know, growing up in my part of the city was never dull. Even the bad things brought an excitement that livened up the day-to-day drudgery of my mother making ends meet, of me fighting my way through that hard, ugly school, because she told me it was my ticket to living better. So when we had a fire, even though it scared me to death, I'd be running out there with everyone else to watch the red engine, the men in back, all the commotion. The howling sirens, that burning smoky smell wasn't all bad, for me. And those men in black, they were heroes. Time after time they'd save a neighbor, a schoolmate, someone's family or dog. It made me live my little life on a higher plane for a few hours, thinking how those people had gotten a second chance, dreaming how I'd live my second chance, this day here." LilyAnn, dark eyes full of light, joked as if to cover up her high ideals. "How if I could save lives like that people might even be glad, for once, I'd been born so tall. I *knew* there had to be a reason I stuck out like the Chrysler building in a bunch of tenements."

They'd drunk a half bottle of wine with dinner, and Sally found herself loving LilyAnn Lee, feeling close and trusting. She lay her hand on LilyAnn's firm arm and told her about Liz's brownstone, and Hanukkah. "It's okay with me if she goes,"

Sally concluded. "I *expect* to be left out. I'm not real family, I'm not the right religion, and it's one of those things you swallow when you're queer."

"Swallow? If you're swallowing it so easily, why are you crying?"

"Because of Liz. She's always making me have emotions." She dried her eyes with a paper napkin. It hadn't really been a cry, just a few wine-induced tears.

"*Making* you have emotions?"

She nodded. "I'm fine on my own. But she's always asking what I feel."

LilyAnn was looking strangely at her. "You know you're talking shit, don't you, girl? You sound like Jefferson," she said, "back when she thought she was a mental Hercules. Nothing reached her. Not cheating on her girl to get me, not bringing me out and then dumping me when she was done, not smashing herself in that car accident. Took me a long time to see her trick. She drowned it all in the juice. What do you do with your feelings, Sal?"

"You mean you think Liz is right? I do feel more than I know I do?"

The waitress brought them each a tortoni, but food no longer appealed to Sally. "Inside," she said, after a silence, "I guess I agree with Liz's dad. It's his home. He doesn't want an outsider there, sharing in an intimate family ritual. Even if I were a man, I'd still be as outsider as you can get."

"Now," LilyAnn said between bites, "thanks to you I

148

know how *he* feels, but I still don't know what you're feeling."

"But I don't *care*." She passed her dessert across the table.

LilyAnn took a break between portions. She stretched her legs into the aisle of the emptying restaurant and locked her hands behind her head. "I am remembering," LilyAnn began in a trance-like voice, "remembering what it felt like when I thought I was an outsider."

"You don't feel like an outsider anymore?"

"A miracle, isn't it? In this long black body of mine. In this queerness that I love. No, I don't feel sad any more, almost ever. I don't feel at the mercy of anyone else's emotions—my mother muttering into her glass how hard life is, my teachers' frustration with how we ghetto kids didn't learn the way we s'posed to, my friends' rage at not being able to have what they wanted in this white world. I stayed an outsider as long as they counted more than I did. When I learned, right after Jefferson left me, to be my own friend, to reach inside me, I became an insider. Life opened up. It's a big thing, life. And I want to stuff as much into it as I can. If somebody doesn't want me around, that's his problem, he's the outsider."

They paid the check and went into the night. "I don't want to go back yet," Sally said. So they walked up to Greenwich Village, past the brightly lit shops, the music spilling from dark clubs, through the noise of panhandlers, drug dealers, tourists and oblivious natives. It felt warmer in the heat of the Village, in the midst of so many smells, expresso, pizza, marijuana, sandalwood incense. "So *that's* how I feel, like an outsider," Sally said.

"I'd stare at those big red trucks," LilyAnn responded, "and the men with their equipment, their know-how, their *guts* and belief in life, everyone's life, and I'd think, back when I was an outsider, I'll never be able to do that."

"I know that feeling. You don't count. If the Chief of the Fire Department doesn't think you belong—"

"If Liz's father doesn't think you belong—"

Sally stopped at an alleyway. "But I *don't* want to go to the brownstone for Hanukkah. I *don't* want to feel like a sore thumb, an intruder, an unbeliever."

"So don't."

"Oh," said Sally, looking into LilyAnn's eyes, and then up the alleyway as if she'd just found the path she'd been looking for. "Oh," she said again. "So *that's* what I really want—not to go. But I do want to share the holy days with Liz. They're part of her, part of us. Even her parents, we need to share them too."

They began walking back, south.

LilyAnn remained silent.

"I *want* to be included in her celebration. That's why I always give her presents. If only there were a way to equalize her parents and me. So it's not all in their ballpark. So I belong too. I want to be able to enjoy what we do share, not feel awful about it."

LilyAnn lay an arm across her shoulders and gave her a sideways hug as they walked. "*That's* a Jefferson Squeeze, hold the lime," LilyAnn said, laughing.

Sunday, as part of the compromise she worked out with her family, Liz went to celebrate the first night of Hanukkah at her parents' brownstone—without Sally.

But the second night, Monday, when the bar was closed, her family kept its part of the bargain and visited Café Femmes to light two of the candles in Liz and Sally's menorah. Liz had invited Gabby, who darted in after her doctor's visit, and LilyAnn Lee, on her way to work, in uniform.

"What, the fire department?" asked Mr. Marks. "I *knew* it must be against some code to light Hanukkah candles in a bar." He was white-haired, with Liz's dark eyes, but his thick still-black eyebrows made him fierce-looking.

"Just don't let me hear the word *shiksa* out of his mouth," Liz had muttered to Sally. She'd come back to work from Brooklyn on Sunday, relieved it was over, that first meeting with her father, full of hope and anger all at the same time. Tonight she wore the long velveteen skirt she saved for weddings and funerals. Sally wore a pantsuit from her days in an office and could hardly breathe. Gabby had chosen her best black overalls and a bright pink shirt.

At last Sally was hearing the fabled interchanges in person.

"*You* gave her a goy name—Elizabeth," accused Mr. Marks in an undertone.

"Quiet, Abe. *You* wanted her to fit in the modern world," Mrs. Marks whispered loudly.

"Not *this* modern."

Liz had made coffee for the baked goods her mother brought.

Its smell, as well as the parents, transformed the bar into something close in intent to what Liz had always said she wanted it to be, but at the same time not as close because of the nervous energy gathered in the air. As they assembled to light the candles there was a knock at the door.

"Closed!" shouted Mr. Marks, obviously on edge.

Liz winced.

"It's probably Amaretto," Gabby said, bustling to the door to let her in.

"What happened?" Amaretto cried, gathering Gabby into her arms. Amaretto's grandmother, Nanny, who spent a great deal of time with the couple, had come in behind her granddaughter. "What did Dr. Sterne have to say?" Amaretto demanded.

Sally felt herself shrink. The last thing they needed in front of Liz's parents was this display of lesbian affection.

Gabby looked toward Liz as if to apologize.

"Gabby had heart tests, Ma, Dad," Liz explained. "She came here straight from the doctor's."

"So why didn't she say right away?" Mrs. Marks asked. "We're some kind of monsters?"

Gabby hung her head. Pretty Amaretto, in her thrift store fake fur, kept an arm around her lover's shoulder. "I don't think—" Gabby said.

"Tell!" bellowed Mr. Marks. He lowered his voice. "I have a little heart problem myself."

"I'm okay. I have 'premature systoles,'" Gabby said with

labored pronunciation. "That's extra heartbeats." Amaretto grabbed her in a hug again.

"That's exactly what I have," said Mr. Marks. "Not to worry," he said reassuringly. "So long as you take care of yourself and keep healthy. Don't drink," he warned, naming preventive measures on stumpy fingers. "Exercise, don't smoke, and," he poked the last finger toward her stomach, "Maybe lose a little weight?"

Gabby laughed. "That's the cheapest second opinion I could have gotten!"

They shook hands. Gabby introduced him to Amaretto and Nanny. Sally looked at Liz, than at LilyAnn Lee in amazement as Gabby and Mr. Marks talked on about their symptoms. Amaretto was still holding Gabby's hand. They'd only been lovers since October and were obviously crazy about each other. Was that why Mrs. Marks went to stand by her husband, and took his hand too? Soon Nanny engaged her in conversation. Mr. Marks glanced down as he talked, looking at his fingers interlaced with his wife's. Then over to Gabby and Amaretto's hands. Then to Nanny, beaming and nodding, apparently completely comfortable. He scratched his chin.

"Okay, okay," said Liz, before her father had a chance to decide he didn't want to be a part of it all. "Did you two come to light the candles or to hang out in our bar all night?"

Everyone laughed.

Liz handed a box of matches to her father.

"Wait!" cried Gabby. She skipped over to the jukebox and

fussed with it briefly. In a moment the room filled with the sounds of "Sunrise, Sunset" from *Fiddler on the Roof*.

"Oy," said Liz.

"Tacky, little Gab," said LilyAnn. "Very tacky."

"Huh?"

LilyAnn folded her arms. "Would you come to my family celebration and play *Porgy and Bess*?"

"It's okay, it's okay," said Mr. Marks. "Let her celebrate her good health any way she wants. Maybe Mrs. Marks will teach you the hora. Good exercise."

Gabby's face was red, but she said, "I want to feel the spirit. This isn't a funeral, it's a holiday! What's a holiday without music? After this scare, I want *everything* to count for me."

Laughing with the rest, Mr. Marks turned to the candles. "This is not the real thing," he began. "It's a little bit ecumenical. So you can understand." The others ranged around the bar. "At Hanukkah the Jews celebrate their freedom to worship. No, we celebrate freedom of religion. For everyone." He gestured toward them all.

Sally's hand stole to Liz's. They were here, all of them, because Sally had decided, and said, it was what she wanted. Liz had thought Hanukkah at the bar was a fantastic idea. And now it felt so good. She needed to touch Liz's soft hand and feel close. She reminded herself there was nothing wrong with showing what she felt.

Mr. Marks went on. "As we light each candle, we symbolize the growth of faith. Always, my wife and I, we have prayed to be

154

reunited with our child, Elizabeth. Life is too short, like Gabby said, to lose anything we have." He reached out his hand to his daughter and she moved toward him, still holding Sally's hand, pulling her along. Sally balked. Liz tugged. Mr. Mark's hand wavered, began to drop, but after Liz's mother jerked obviously at his coat, he steadied the hand, pulled Liz, and Sally, to himself. "Always, my God humbles me, teaches me through His will," Mr. Marks said, head bowed.

Then he looked up at Liz, and for the first time, at Sally. She imagined this time she really did look pale, like Friday when LilyAnn teased her. But LilyAnn wouldn't say a thing, she knew, because she had seen the tears rolling down those broad brown cheeks. It made her want to cry too. She swallowed hard.

"Once more then," said Mr. Marks, "as at the first Hanukkah, we celebrate a miracle of faith." He turned, said some words in Hebrew and lit the two candles.

"Tomorrow," he said then, turning back to Liz and Sally, "will you both," and his voice sounded choked here, as if the word *both* came hard, very hard, "will you both come for the lighting, to Brooklyn?"

"If we can cover the bar," Sally answered, stopping herself from obsequiously thanking him for his acceptance. She wanted an out should she choose to use it.

After coffee and pastries, her parents hugged her and shook hands all around. Outside, Liz walked them to their car. Sally stood just beyond Café Femmes' awning, looking up. The temperature had risen and the puffy snow clouds were gone for now. The sky would weep another day.

She stubbornly kept her eyes skyward as LilyAnn joined her. It wouldn't do to look down and let all those tears fall out of her eyes. But then LilyAnn Lee put an arm around her shoulder and squeezed her tight. Sally, feeling like a cloud whose time has come, looked wetly down.

# FIRES OF WINTER SOLSTICE

## Lee Lynch

The fire, thought LilyAnn Lee, who was six feet tall even without her firefighters' boots, could have been worse. A big old warehouse full of furniture, an alert little watchman who'd smelled the smoke despite the flask in his pocket.

It had been clear to her right away from the smell and pattern that the fire was electrical in origin, so as soon as they'd controlled the flames, they began the tedious job of finding where it had started, making certain it spread no further. This was the kind of work that demanded only half of LilyAnn's mind. She drifted above the garbagey wet smoke smell, above the splintered furniture, above her light on the wall as she excavated for signs of burning wiring.

Now and then a distinct whiff of burnt cedar reached her from that stack of hope chests she and Horrigan had wet down for fear of sparks. A smell like the cedar they'd burned in Alley Pond Park last year for the Solstice Ritual. Her friends from the Women's Food Co-op had been urging her to return this year, but damn, she'd been so uncomfortable.

All those white girls, she thought, those earnest women with their dead-serious incantation of the Goddess. There was something so thin and pale about their very ceremony. They gathered in circles like doubting but hopeful supplicants who prayed extra hard to get past a sense of make-believe. The woman who'd learned rituals on the west coast seemed intense and desperate, determined to perform her office exactly right, not to let any wavering spirit she called on flee in the tendrils of smoke that rose from the tiny illicit fire in the park. She wondered if Dawn and Goldie, the other sisters who'd been there, felt strange too. Would they go back into the night to sit in this year's cold circle?

She remembered, as she worked along the wall and checked periodically on big beefy Horrigan across from her, the promise of light in the women's song.

> You can't kill the spirit
> She's like a mountain
> Bold and strong
> She goes on and on.

It was getting smoky again. Had Horrigan found something? She couldn't see its source. She put her mask on, breathing easier, seeing somewhat better, and waved to Horrigan, who didn't seem bothered by the smoke yet and ignored her signal. He was a temporary partner, an old-timer whose regular partner, like hers, was on vacation. Horrigan was a bigot, but close enough to retirement not to buck this pairing with a black "fire impersonator," as he called the women in the department.

She peered through the smoke to the wires she followed. Upstairs more of the company searched, heavy-booted, as carefully as she. Sometimes she felt closer to these guys her life depended on than to the women at the Co-op. She partied with the women, sat in meetings with them, joined their ritual circles, but that click wasn't there, the click of bonding in the face of danger.

While she was drawn to women's spirituality, found it closer than anything else she could accept, it didn't feel anywhere as meaningful as the mass prayer at a firefighter's funeral or the firehouse Christmas tree. Didn't warm her even as much as the static-filled radio insistently filling their living quarters with carols. All the fire fighters, women and men, talked bah-humbug and complained about Christmas Day duty, but the women brought in baked goods, the guys gave out cartons of cigarettes or quarts of liquor.

LilyAnn had made a ritual of reporting for her Christmas shift early with four uncooked mince pies and cooking them right there, filling the firehouse with their smell. Last year a false alarm had come in while they baked. LilyAnn had forgotten the pies until the truck was halfway back to the firehouse.

She'd raced up to the oven. Someone had gauged when the pies were done and turned the oven off, but she'd never been able to find out who.

She was chanting to herself as she worked.

> You can't kill the spirit
> She's like a mountain
> Bold and strong
> She goes on and on.

Her back ached from holding her arms up, the backs of her legs were beginning to tremble from the strain of walking sideways in a crouch, the mask was biting into her face, which had swelled from the heat.

She worked methodically on. Crazy things happened in these old buildings: fire just waiting to explode out of a wall where it was trapped, beams so weak the heat and water sent them crashing through the ceiling below. Horrigan was masked now too—professional, thorough, like her. He'd probably dragged many a black woman from a burning building. She hoped again that she could rely on him to rescue one more, even, she smiled to herself, if she was an unwelcome peer.

Unlike at Alley Pond where she, Goldie and Dawn were welcomed warmly, treated with respect, even wooed by the white women who'd learned that a healthy culture was an inclusive one. How the burnt cedar smell pulled her back to that night, helped her see that some part of herself longed for, belonged with the women as they lit their candles to light the way through whatever winter brought.

They'd used the cedar for purification, burned it carefully, with sentries posted, knowing full well that discovery meant more than a fine for their little bonfire surrounded by buckets of water. Celebrating the Solstice was pagan; the police or the media could choose to make much of it. Were there still laws on the books against witchcraft?

Her rebellious self would return to the fire circle for certain. Hadn't her people, after all, been as defiant? They'd salvaged their African fires and chants, bits and pieces anyway, from the puritanical wrath they found on these shores. In the Solstice circle she'd sat cross-legged, butt cold against the ground, feeling the souls of those ancestors swell and fill and heat her own body till she felt like a great Amazon warrior, one of many, many daughters of daughters, gargantuan and powerful. Was this fantasy or memory, she'd wondered. Hadn't the Amazons come from Africa, been dark-skinned?

> You can't kill the spirit
> She's like a mountain
> Bold and strong
> She goes on and on.

The warehouse was silent but for the shuffling boots. She felt as if she were mining the world for light and heat, a lot more of both than the women's candles gave. The priestess had instructed each woman to light the candle of the woman to her left, and to address the topic of power when the light reached her. How they'd gather power to warm themselves, arm themselves against the frozen wasteland of the patriarchy.

Well, here I am, thought LilyAnn, working with that very patriarchal beast, sure hot enough now. Sweat ran down her face under the mask. She couldn't mop it with her fire-retardant sleeve. Was the work making her hotter, or was she nearing a hidden fire?

She couldn't survive that African sun now, she decided. Her blood had changed. Where did she belong—the cold park, the hot warehouse, neither? The men stomped and chopped, getting noisy with frustration as they searched for fires that might not be there.

"You can't kill the spirit," the women had chanted. But even Goldie and Dawn had looked drawn and weak, and their voices had sounded quavery. Did LilyAnn want a spirit like she'd seen in church? One that would so move woman after woman that they'd flare into words or song and testify its strength? *Something*, anything but polite turn-taking, awkwardly recited words. It seemed that she, along with the others, chipped and chipped away at the wall between them and their spirituality, bit by bit, cut into the plaster that help them back.

Fire makes a sound like a great gulp when it finds enough oxygen to swallow. LilyAnn leapt back from the box-sized inferno that exploded at her. Her sweat was gone. Her training, like a blind faith, took her over. She quickly, distinctly, told her

162

radio she needed help even as she turned to summon Horrigan. He'd heard the great gulp, though, and had begun his run across to her when another dreaded sound filled her ears. A crack, a tearing, a "Whoa!" of surprise as Horrigan crashed through the floor.

So close to retirement, LilyAnn thought, and turned her back to the spreading flames. She ran along what she'd later picture as a wall of candle—the flames reflected in her mask's eyepiece—toward Horrigan who hung over the deep basement below. Cold air gusted up toward the flames, drawn like the firefighters who she could hear rushing to contain them. She gave them the flames like gifts, trusting their skills.

Earlier she'd noted the placement of posts in the huge room and now ran to one, attached her rope, then treaded softly to the edges of the cold hole. She was big, but lighter than a running man. She prayed to the Goddess that the edge would hold as she lay, belly down, to crawl and stretch until she reached Horrigan.

> She's like a mountain
> Bold and strong
> She goes on and on.

Damn, she thought as she attached the two rings which must hold Horrigan's weight, damn if that vision of herself as an Amazon didn't come back to make her feel trebly strong. And damn, she thought again as Horrigan heaved himself finally over the edge and they scuttled away from the weak floor—damn if that wall of candles wasn't there in her head to guide them though the thick smoke to safety.

They both grabbed hoses and helped drag them in, then trained them on the fire. The hoses were bonds she could see, linking them against danger. Yet the circle whose spirit she hadn't been able to see, touch, believe, had been there for her too, a song that moved with her, that moved her. She'd never expected to feel the joy that tingled everywhere inside her now in this rank-smelling fire site. And she'd never expected Horrigan's words, behind her on the hose.

"For a minute," he shouted, mask pushed aside, "I thought I might not be around this year to save your mince pies."

# THE GIFT

# Katherine V. Forrest

The Tehachapi mountains had been selected for the rendez-vous. Behind Marge Bowman and Karla Cooper lay the high-rise glitter of Los Angeles; ahead, the humble lights of Bakersfield. The Winter Solstice night was cool, crystalline, the stars abundant and close, the summer smell of cooling earth rich and vivid.

The two women had been in their designated place since six o'clock, only two hours early for the rendezvous; but they had come from Oregon—not nearly so far as the other parents—to this single site in the United States, one of ten around the globe. Thousands of parents were gathered along the foothills, but only intermittent murmurs of voices nearby reached Marge and Karla.

Marge pointed a trembling finger at the TV display. "Julie looks so frightened."

Karla did not glance at the screen; through binoculars she stared at the floodlit plain below. She shifted the glasses from the spaceship, pulsing its midnight blue rhythms several miles away, over the thousands of tiny figures populating the plain, to their daughter's compound. "The Monitors are doing their best. Soon it'll be over. Soon, Margie."

Marge said more calmly, "It's going to be worse when the Monitors leave, when it . . . happens."

"Margie, I know," she said helplessly. "I know."

On the screen before Marge Bowman, in slow pan over the children in compound 20D, the remote-controlled camera picked up the face of their daughter—pale, frightened, her blonde silk hair blowing in the cool breeze flowing over the plain. Julie was wearing a warm jacket and pants, but she had apparently lost or discarded her cap. She scanned the plain anxiously, staring at the mountains toward Marge, then twisted to gaze at the distant blinking ship. The Monitor, a young woman in a belted white suit with a red band on the sleeve, came to Julie, knelt and encircled her with an arm.

Marge gazed at her sturdy, beautiful daughter. Julie had been born prematurely—but physically perfect—and had always been small, and beautiful. Unusually beautiful, all the doctors had agreed. Julie hugged the Monitor, her smile radiant; as the camera panned past her, she looked into the lens with wide, vacant blue eyes.

Only one month ago they had met with the Western Director of *Project Transfer*. "Four to seven are the optimum ages, the highest probability—they've established that conclusively," Doctor Morton had told them. "Any younger, the child is too unformed to withstand the shock, the pain. Any older, the biological changes will have destroyed the compatibility. Consequently, Julie will never have another chance."

"The pain," Marge Bowman had said.

"The pain will be extreme. To the farthest limit of tolerance. The process involves imprinting upon the neurological system, and the Mirilians have told us the children cannot be tranquilized. There is no other way. There is nothing to be done about the pain. Talk to the psychologists, the scientists working on the project. Marge, Karla, you have one month to decide whether you want your child to be part of *Project Transfer*. One month."

Karla watched her daughter; watched her pull the hair of a boy of perhaps five with red curls, who whirled to Julie. Julie hugged him, laughing.

Karla whispered, "I love her so. Oh God, how I love her."

Staring at the screen, Marge murmured, "I don't know ... I just don't know ..."

"Margie, we've discussed it. Decided." But Karla's voice was tired; and she was uncertain, even now.

"Look." Marge pointed at the screen.

In compound 20D, a Monitor, a dark-haired young woman, was gently and carefully tucking a small, crying boy into a gaily colored conveyance that looked like a toy helicopter. The

Monitor straightened, raised both arms; the remote-controlled toy-like copter rose, soared toward Marge and Karla and the mountains.

"See?" Marge said. "Another recall, there've been *dozens*, Karla. Lots of other parents are changing their minds. We can too. There's still time, right up to . . . the moment."

"Is there anything we haven't gone over?" Karla's fingers traced, circled the recall button on the TV console. "If there's a conceivable reason to change our minds, let's give the signal—have the Monitors return Julie to us."

But there was no reason they hadn't discussed. Endlessly. Exhaustively. They had argued with all the psychologists, the scientists. Talked with each other late into the nights. Awakened at predawn hours to talk still more. Karla could not now remember which objections each had raised, who of them had answered:

"She's our only child, both of us are too old to conceive another."

"For that very reason we owe her whatever we can give—the best springboard possible for her life."

"It's dangerous. It's never been done before."

"The Mirilians are advanced far beyond us. Look at their technology, what they've already given us as a gesture of good will. They tell us it's eighty percent probability—and they're risking their own children, too."

"They also tell us there's a ten percent chance of insanity. A ten percent chance Julie may die."

"But an eighty percent chance for success. A *good* chance. Her *only* chance."

"God gave her to us the way she is, with her limitations."

"The children of Mirilius, are they not also God's creatures?"

"But we love her the way she is ... Maybe we love her more ..."

"Are we thinking of Julie, or ourselves?"

On the screen Julie was again looking toward the mountains—toward Marge and Karla—with frightened, bewildered eyes.

The loving sweetness of my daughter, Karla thought. The way she can almost tear the heart out of my chest ... She'll be forever changed ... "Why is it taking so long," she demanded in a surge of anger. "Their ship's been here more than an hour. How long do they think we can keep thousands of children calm?"

"Karla, they're doing what we had to do. Saying goodbye to their own children."

But at first, Marge reflected, it had been hard to ascribe feelings to the Mirilians. What they looked like—*that* had taken some getting used to.

The scientists, candid about all aspects of the project, had shown both women holographs of a huge lethal planet of methane and fluoride, and its inhabitants: awesome creatures, easily dominant on their world, stork-like, with one huge green eye, a cruel predatory beak, an immense torso, two powerful limbs that propelled them at breakneck speed over their forbidding terrain.

Dr. Francona had said, "The one essential they have in common with us is love for their young—even more so than we. Mistreatment of offspring is inconceivable. Love for their young is their single greatest outpouring of racial psychic energy, the highest value in their culture."

The psychologist had said, "The Mirilians are completely dissimilar biologically, but they discovered during visits over the last three centuries that the neural structure and circuitry of our bodies and theirs is virtually identical in the first stages of life.

"The greatest tragedy on their world is an infant born physically damaged. It is doomed. On Mirilius, there are no *degrees* of health as we know it. The body of a damaged infant withers and dies, dissolved by their pitiless atmosphere. But only the body dies. The infant metamorphoses into this."

Dr. Francona displayed another holograph to Marge and Karla, cross-shaped spokes of light, ice blue and glowing with energy. "To us this looks like electricity. But it's life, and intelligence. But life doesn't last very long—less than one of our Earth years. With the dawning and growth of intelligence, the infant becomes fully aware of its loss, and grieves and longs for a physical body. The infant eventually relinquishes its will to live."

The scientist had said, "The Mirilians have visited us several times earlier in our history—in the ninth and sixteenth centuries as well as the last three. They're appalled by our history and culture, and would never have made themselves known to us except for their discovery about our children. But they'll return every year if this project is successful, to share more of their knowledge and to continue the project. They have decided to take a chance on us by trusting us with their greatest value—their children."

The screen Marge was watching flashed red. A soft voice announced: "The signal has come from the Mirilian ship. Two minutes."

Through the binoculars, Karla watched the fine blonde hair blow across the forehead of her daughter. She lowered the glasses and swallowed. Tears blurred her vision.

Marge watched the screen; the Monitor knelt beside Julie, hugged her sturdy shoulders, smiled goodbye. Then the Monitor stood, touched a stud on the belt of her white suit. Julie and the other children stared open-mouthed as she floated upward, joined hundreds of other Monitors who drifted gracefully over the plain to the slopes of the mountains, wingless white birds propelled by gravibelt, a gift from the Mirilians.

An opening appeared in the side of the Mirilian ship, a dazzling brilliance in the dark night.

"Karla," Marge whispered.

She flung her arms around Marge; they stood watching, not the screen, but the vast floodlit plain below crowded with Earth children.

Spokes of electric blue light poured from the ship, became wheels of blue flame whirling over the flat plain at incredible speeds under the star-flung sky. From the plain, from the thousands of milling children, rose faint cries.

Karla's eyes were drawn irresistibly to the screen. Amid the terrorized children in compound 20D, Julie stood rooted, hypnotized by horror, mouth open in a scream, not heeding the glancing blow from the boy with red hair who ran into her as he fled the onrushing spokes of blue light.

"Julie," Karla said. She suddenly shouted, "No! Not Julie!"

From all around them came moans and cries of other parents as the fiery blue spokes of light overran the plain, bounced and careened over the Earth children, engulfed them. Shrieks of agony rose into the crystal night air.

"Karla! Oh God!" Marge's eyes were riveted to the screen where her daughter was seized in blue light, her body rigid and quivering, her hair an electrified blonde halo. Her eyes wide with agony and terror, she mouthed the words Mama Mama. Marge tore herself from Karla's arms and ran.

Karla leaped after her, grasped her shoulders, dragged her back. "There's nothing we can do!"

Clinging to each other, they watched their daughter writhe and twist in the devouring blue flame.

Gradually, slowly, the blue dimmed, faded, died. Julie and all the children near her slumped to the ground, limbs twitching. Then they lay still, utterly motionless.

"She's dead." Karla's voice was toneless. "It didn't work. We killed her. We've killed our children and theirs too." She released Marge, turned from the sight of the deathly still little figures. The gamble had been lost. Why ever had they risked the one great treasure in their lives?

"No, Karla. Look."

The children were stirring. Soon Julie shook her head, rolled over, sat up, looked at the children around her who were also sitting up and staring at each other and down at themselves. Julie looked at her hands, turned them over and back, examining them. She plucked at her clothing, touched the clothing of the black girl next to her. The black girl stood, took a tentative step, stumbled, kept her balance. Julie got up, facing the mountains, but looking down at her feet—and tumbled to the ground. The black girl reached for Julie's hands, pulled her up. Carefully, Julie placed one foot in front of the other, arms extended for balance. Several minutes later she was walking with grace and ease. She tried a clumsy trot, joined hands with the black girl, and ran in an awkward circle. Children all around them joined hands, ran back and forth. From the plain rose the treble of children, voices screaming, shrieking with joy.

"Julie," breathed Marge Bowman.

Karla Cooper knelt to her seven-year-old daughter, took the small hands in hers and looked into her eyes.

Blue eyes looked back into hers with awareness; they contained what all the doctors, all the neurologists, all the genetics experts had said was forever impossible for their retarded child: intelligence.

Julie Bowman-Cooper spoke. "I know only these Earth

words until you teach me more." She spoke in a childish lisp, but without a trace of the speech dysfunction that had always caused her to slur her words. "My natal beings who cherish me wish to thank you."

Marge Bowman lifted her eyes to the spaceship which was rising slowly from the surface of the Earth, on its way back to the lonely stars.

"Thank you," she whispered. "We'll do our very best."

# SIGHTSEERS IN DEATH VALLEY

## Jane Rule

Driving into Death Valley at Christmas time—the time of year it was first discovered by white men—is something like arriving in a place only months after it has been bombed. The disaster here, of course, is simply summer with its hundred-and-twenty-degree heat, its infrequent but violent rains, its windstorms. Permanent signs along the main roads give directions for driving in the desert, for survival. Neither whiskey nor urine is a real substitute for water. Temporary signs indicate which roads are closed, buried in sand drifts, or washed out by flash floods. It is a fragile land, a weatherbed reformed by any caprice of the wind, for very little grows here except desert holly and mesquite, and on the sand dunes even those disappear, as they do also in the salt flats where only the crystals themselves grow, pushing up through the silt surface in arthritic gestures.

By now, though the signs of summer desecration are everywhere, the air is cool and still. The mountains, barren, exposing geological violence as remotely slow-moving as the wind is swift, are nearly gaudy under the winter sun, red, blue green, violet, yellow. The desert holly is in bloom with small outcroppings the color of blood. At the inn it has been tied with red ribbon and put on every door.

The population of the valley is at its largest this time of year, and its makeup is similar to those of other sunny Christmas resorts. Many Jewish families are trying to save their children from the disaster of Christmas itself. A number of young grandparents are still struggling to recover rather than swallow pride after the first rift with young in-laws. Childless couples with two incomes can afford a winter holiday. Single women in groups of three are too old to keep going home for Christmas, and an occasional couple, lesbian, perhaps can't. A few whole Christian families, including teen-aged children and grandparents, are affluent enough to celebrate Christmas away from home. The very old, escaping winter, need the sun and the hot springs more than great-grandparental joy.

Like most places, there is lots to do or nothing. Children can ride hard-mouthed, exhausted little horses that walk into and out of Breakfast Canyon once a day, bully a parent into going to the swimming pool, play volleyball, shuffleboat. There is an eighteen-hole golf course. There are two museums. In the evening there is dancing, a movie, a slide show, a naturalist's talk. For the campers any place that is warm and light for those first early hours of the winter night is a good place. The ranch saloon usually closes at nine-thirty instead of the advertised midnight because only employees are still drinking along with Sky King, a little man in a cowboy hat who flies charters into the Grand Canyon or sells tickets to the movie. No place is crowded. Nobody is rowdy. People who want real night life are in Las Vegas.

At the ranch swimming pool, there is a large sign which says, NO LIFEGUARD IS ON DUTY. The handsome man who is obviously paid to sit there reads a book or talks to the guests. If he missed a drowning, he'd only be obeying the sign. Miss Jensen, whose friend has taken to the horses, is reading T.S. Eliot. Mrs. Dirkheimer, whose five-year-old son has whined his father into a game of shuffleboard, stares at Miss Jensen.

"Do you just like T.S. Eliot?"

"Heavens no," Miss Jensen answers. "I teach him."

"My husband is interested in literature," Mrs. Dirkheimer says. "As a hobby."

"I breed bulldogs," Miss Jensen says, a lie which will allow her to go on reading.

Miss Jensen is not fond of animals, even human animals, but she has a large amount of passive tolerance. Later in the day she will find her friend, and they will collect rocks, which make the best companions.

Marne Ginter is saying to Alice Faymoor, "Christmas with kids just turns into gimme, gimme, gimme. So I said to

Maureen, 'Don't worry about us. You and Joe and the kids go ahead and do your own thing. We're taking a vacation.' 'A vacation!' she says, 'At this time of year? People'll think we had a fight or something.' 'Well, so, is truth going to hurt them?' I said. 'But where are you going to go at Christmas?' 'Death Valley,' I said. Do you know, she started crying?"

Marne and Alice are laughing. The sun is hot. Today isn't Christmas.

"Listen, Hymen," his father says to the three-year-old retching into the trough, "if you go under the water and you breathe, you'll drown and die. How many times do I have to tell you? You'll drown and die."

"How?" Hymen asks.

"What do you mean, *how*?"

"The kid wants a demonstration," another father calls. It's Dirkheimer, back from five long minutes of shuffleboard. "I'd like to give him one with my kid."

"You irritating your father?" young Mrs. Dirkheimer demands.

"Naw, he's not. I'm only speaking in the interests of science."

"Did you thank your father for playing shuffleboard with you? Did you?"

Miss Jensen closes her book, folds up her sunglasses, and puts on her white terry-cloth robe.

"Aren't you going in today?" the non-lifeguard asks.

"I've been," Miss Jensen answers, smiling.

"Hymen! Holy God ..."

Hymen is retching into the trough again. He'll be swimming or dead by tomorrow.

"That woman," Dirkheimer's wife is saying, "breeds bull-dogs."

"You're kidding me."

"She said so herself."

They stare after Miss Jensen, who's forty if she's a day, never mind she's watched her figure.

"Well, you gotta have human pity," Dirkheimer says.

A nubile champion goes off the diving board while men watch in uncertain, parental lechery, except for the paid attendant, who is now reading *The Nakcd Ape.*

"For laughs," he explains when Marne Ginter asks, as she and Alice walk by to meet their golf-playing husbands for lunch.

"He's a good case for skin cancer," Alice says. "If you ask me."

"I never liked a conceited man. That's what I don't understand about Maureen. To marry a guy like that. He is like that, Joe is. Just plain conceited."

Though Scotty's Castle is a good two-hour drive north from the oasis of the ranch and inn, Miss Jensen and her friend discover it is not an outing for escaping the others. On their way there, they sight Dirkheimer coming over a sand dune on his knees with his tongue hanging out for his wife to take a picture, their five-year-old standing at a puzzled distance.

"He must cake Tums," the friend observes. "His tongue is white."

"Probably the food in the cafeteria doesn't agree with him," Miss Jensen suggests.

They have brought their own food and electric pans, which they keep hidden behind the stock of towels in the bathroom. There is no sign in the cabin forbidding cooking, but since there is no provision for it they have decided to be careful rather than to inquire.

Farther along they catch sight of the Ginters and Faymoors, who are collecting desert holly in a rocky field beside the road. Miss Jensen's friend notes with pleasure Marne Ginter's orange blouse, Alice Faymoor's aquamarine, colors attractive against the nearly subtle mountains.

"People ought to dress not only for the weather but for the landscape."

"It's against the law to pick that holly."

"Well, we're not rangers," Miss Jensen's friend replies, holiday relief in her voice.

When they arrive at Scotty's Castle, the man who is not a lifeguard at the pool is already there with an older man the women have not seen before. His Mercedes suggests he is staying at the inn, which costs at least double what it does at the ranch, with no way to avoid the dining room for meals. Miss Jensen and her friend have booked there for Christmas dinner.

The younger man smiles at Miss Jensen.

"He's got to be quite a buddy of yours," her friend observes.

"He's one of us," Miss Jensen replies.

"Isn't he just!"

Shortly the Dirkheimers, Ginters, and Faymoors all arrive, and they begin the tour of this unlikely, not mysterious enough whim of a man of uncertain taste.

"No worse than Longleat," Miss Jensen's friend observes, a comparison so absurd Miss Jensen laughs.

"I'm not crazy about all this Indian and Mexican stuff, are you?" Marne is asking Alice.

"Most of it looks as if it ought to be in a church," Alice says. "A *Catholic* church." They both giggle.

Alice's husband lights a cigarette and is asked to put it out. He is perfectly pleasant about it but after that he yawns a lot; and as they approach the much heralded music room, he begins to sigh. Ginter offers him a piece of gum, which he refuses.

"Hymen, you can't go up there, it's roped off," a familiar father's voice orders.

"I thought that kid was drowned yesterday," Dirkheimer says quietly to his wife, while increasing the pressure on his own obedient son's hand.

Though the music room is large for a private house, the tourists are too numerous for the seats. The two men give up their seats for Miss Jensen and her friend.

"Show," Marne says. "For some men that's all there is."

The organ is badly asthmatic. Miss Jensen and her friend suffer for Bach. Alice and Marne stifle laughter. Dirkheimer wonders if he ought to offer to try to fix it. He built an electric organ once from a kit. Hymen begins to cry.

"At least we're not all on the same bus," Miss Jensen observes as they walk into the parking lot.

"It would have saved gas," her friend answers.

The man with the Mercedes comes up to them and says, "If you're planning to have Christmas dinner at the inn, would you join us for drinks beforehand?"

"Oh, I ..." Miss Jensen hesitates, looking to her friend.

"Why not?" her friend asks lightly.

"About six o'clock then?"

"Thank you," Miss Jensen says.

"Did you see that man in the Mercedes pick up our bulldog breeder back there in the parking lot?" Dirkheimer's wife asks him.

"He didn't pick her up," their five-year-old corrects. "He was just talking to her."

"Maybe he doesn't know her terrible secret," Dirkheimer speculates.

"What's that?" the child demands.

"That she breeds bulldogs."

"That's not a secret!" the child says in disgust and turns out of his parents' silly and incomprehensible conversation.

"That car, that diamond ring, that good-looking lifeguard: he's got to be h-o-m-o-s-e-x-u-a-l."

"Maybe it's a case of birds of a feather," Dirkheimer suggests.

"Not those women!" his wife protests, shocked.

Dirkheimer shrugs over his steering wheel.

Tomorrow he will agree with Hootstein, Hymen's father, to

share the cost of hiring Sky King to fly both families into the Grand Canyon on Christmas Day.

"Hymen will probably throw up the whole way," Dirkheimer's wife protests.

"So I was supposed to say no?" Dirkheimer asks. "You want to play gentile-for-a-day instead?"

There is an enormous and badly decorated Christmas tree in the ranch cafeteria, where Miss Jensen and her friend decide to eat on Christmas Eve since, after a week of cooking out of their cupboard, what is left doesn't seem festive enough for the occasion. There are presents under the tree, which distress the children with impatient greed.

"There's nothing inside them, Hymen," his father explains.

"How do you know?" Hymen demands.

"I know. Take my word for it," his father answers.

"We always have meatloaf at home on Christmas Eve," Marne confides to Alice. "It's a sort of tradition. I wonder if Maureen's made it anyway."

"If I know Joe," her husband says, "they'll be eating steak tonight *and* tomorrow."

"Not on Christmas Day!" Marne protests.

"The guy eats like a truck driver," Ginter complains to the table at large. "Your daughter gets married, and before long you've got to spend a thousand bucks to be sure to get turkey on Christmas Day."

"Or goose," Alice suggests. "I think they're going to have both at the inn."

"Goose!" Ginter says. "Where are we? Merry old England?"

The Faymoors' older son is with his rich in-laws, an every-other-year arrangement in which the Faymoors are not included. Their younger son is somewhere in Europe. They don't even know where to send his presents, which are wrapped up at home in his closet.

The staff is gathering by the Christmas tree, both men and women with big red crepe-paper bows around their necks.

"They're going to sing Christmas carols," Hymen's mother warns, wanting to clap her hands over Hymen's ears.

"It's probably going on even in Jerusalem," Dirkheimer says, preaching resignation.

To their relief and Miss Jensen's disgust the first song is "Rudolph, the Red-Nosed Reindeer." When "I'm Dreaming of a White Christmas" begins, Marne gets up and leaves the cafeteria.

"I don't know," her husband says wearily, getting up to follow her. "She takes things too hard."

"He's got her Cuisinart for Christmas," Alice's husband confides.

"She doesn't have anybody to cook for," Alice says sadly.

On Christmas morning, the sun shines on a dusting of snow on the tops of all the surrounding mountains, from a storm that passed through in the night. The Dirkheimers and Hootsteins are waving to everyone as they start out to the airport. Hymen is wearing swimming goggles to look like a World War I aviator.

"Can't Jews eat turkey?" Marne asks Alice. "There's nothing religious about that, is there?"

"Maybe if they're kosher," Alice suggests doubtfully, as they stroll toward the pool.

"Look," Marne whispers, "the naked ape has a new St. Christopher medal around his neck."

"Santa Claus probably gave it to him," Alice whispers back.

"In his Mercedes," Marne adds, thinking, at least Joe isn't a faggot. Miss Jensen, already at the pool, is again reading T.S. Eliot, "The Journey of the Magi," in honor of the day which will otherwise go unremarked until the evening feast. She and her friend, who is on her morning ride, have given each other a new freezer for the house they share, which was installed before they left for their Death Valley holiday.

*Then at dawn we came down to a temperate valley*
*Wet, below the snow line, smelling of vegetation*

Miss Jensen lifts her eyes to the mountains and thinks, in such a place as this miracles can be expected but are not. She finds it curious that so many of the places Indians chose to live have been left essentially uninhabited by white men. Here the Indians wintered in the valley and retreated into the mountains to escape the heat of summer, a sensible arrangement requiring neither furnace nor air-conditioner, to say nothing of a freezer.

*All that was a long time ago, I remember*

Ginter and Faymoor are joining their wives. Foregoing their golf game is as close to a religious gesture as they will make. They all discuss not phoning their children in elaborate agreement over not being able to get through, over getting through and being handed over to a grandchild too young to talk.

"We'd just make them all jealous," Marne concludes, taking off her robe and stretching out in the sun.

The others study her for gooseflesh. The sun won't really be warm enough for such gestures for another hour.

"At breakfast I heard a woman say she missed cooking Christmas dinner!" Alice offers for laughs.

"I'm going to bust out crying tonight when I don't get to saw away at my very own bird. You know, I don't think I've ever tasted *hot* turkey," Faymoor offers to help the mood along.

"What I think I dislike most about Christmas," Ginter announces in a loud voice, "is that it exists."

"But does it?" the friendly non-lifeguard calls over to him.

Miss Jensen puts down her book and makes slow preparations for her morning swim, involving ear plugs, cap, goggles, and nose clip. This morning, because Hymen isn't there drowning in the way of each turn at the shallow end, she has decided to do a hundred rather than her usual fifty lengths. Since everything today will seem twice as long, she can be willfully cooperative.

"My God," Marne says at Miss Jensen's seventy-fifth turn, "she must be training for the senior Olympics."

The ranch guests going to the inn for dinner have so smartly turned themselves out for the assault on their wealthier neighbors that they hardly recognize their pool and cafeteria companions. Both Marne and Alice are in long dresses, their husbands in ties to match. Miss Jensen is in a black pantsuit, her friend is in white, and the non-lifeguard, who is escorting them, wears a crested jacket.

"He must be a good ten years younger than they are," Marne comments.

"They're probably paying for his dinner," Faymoor suggests.

"Mr. Mercedes is, I'll bet," Alice says.

Mr. Mercedes certainly greets the threesome like a proper host, though he hasn't bothered to put on a tie for the occasion. He's got on a black turtleneck, which makes him look faintly religious. In the crowded bar, he has managed to reserve a table, while the Faymoors and Ginters must choose between standing for a drink and having it in the dining room.

"What it costs you to be one of the cattle!" Ginter complains.

"No room at the inn," Alice shouts gaily.

Miss Jensen is helped into her chair, the poem still in her head.

> *We returned to our places, these Kingdoms*
> *But no longer at ease here in the old dispensation*

Heterosexuality rather than Christianity is the surviving religion here; and she feels, even in the company of these brothers, uncomfortably compromised by it. Briefly she envies the flight of the Jews into the Grand Canyon. Her friend will enjoy the evening as merely exotic. Since Miss Jensen lost her first friend to a combination of fear and boredom, she accepts compromise in defense against such enemies.

In the middle of their first drink, which Mr. Mercedes has ordered by brand, the waiter hands the non-lifeguard a message.

"The little fart!" he cries. "What did he have to do that for?"

"What is it? What's happened?"

"He's crashed that shitty little crate into the salt flats and killed them all!"

The non-lifeguard covers his face and weeps. No one at the table moves or speaks.

"Who?" someone at the next table asks.

"Sky King?" someone else asks.

"I think we'd better go in to dinner," Miss Jensen says. "Thank you for the drink."

"I'm terribly sorry," Miss Jensen's friend says, laying a light hand on the shoulder of the sobbing man.

Miss Jensen takes her arm to urge her away.

"We should never get mixed up with people like that," Miss Jensen whispers, avoiding the questioning faces of the Ginters and the Faymoors.

"He's your friend, not mine!"

"Maybe we could get their table," Marne suggests.

"But what's happened?" Alice asks.

"Air crash," someone says. "Bunch of people killed."

"Sky King," someone else adds.

Mr. Mercedes has also left the table and is moving quickly through the crowd answering nobody's questions.

A waiter is trying to get the unhappy and now solitary man to move.

"Come on, hey? It's Christmas, you know. A lot of people here want to be happy. Come on. You can go out through the back here."

Finally he is persuaded to go.

"I feel really faint," Marne says, sitting down at the vacated table.

"They didn't even want to see the Grand Canyon," Ginter says quietly. "They just wanted to avoid ... this."

"Christmas," Alice says.

"I want to say something," Faymoor announces. "I don't mean to sound hard or anything, but this is our holiday, and we should go on enjoying it, you know?"

"I think maybe we'd better call home," Marne says. "If it's on the news and they don't release names ..."

"Right after dinner," her husband agrees.

In the morning they are all, except the non-lifeguard, gathered in a crowd at Badwater, the lowest point in the valley, two-hundred-eighty feet below sea level, a sign marking where sea level is on a cliff far above their heads. A large flattop truck and a crane are parked waiting, as the crowd is waiting, for a helicopter to come back from the salt flats with the first fragments of the wreck.

"They got the bodies out last night," someone is explaining.

A child says, "Take a picture of the truck, Daddy."

"It's just a truck. This is the lowest place on the continent. Do you realize that? See, that's sea level way up there."

"I want a picture of the truck."

"Maureen said they had meatloaf," Marne is saying to Alice.

"All you had to do was look at that crate to know it wasn't safe," Ginter is saying to Faymoor. "And the pilot was a drunk. All you had to do was look at him ..."

"I want to apologize about last night," Mr. Mercedes was saying to a reluctant Miss Jensen and her friend. "They were good friends. It was a terrible shock for him."

His next words are obscured by the sound of the helicopter, which approaches across the mudflats of Badwater like a great bird of prey, its catch part of the fuselage. As it comes to earth, the wind envelops crowd in a sudden cloud of dust, as if a great conjurer had decided to make them all disappear; but when the fragile dust settles again, they are all still there, watching and talking.

# DALLYING WITH LLAMAS

## Kris Brandenburger

Lost Coast? Llama backpacking? Before I said yes to any such combination I wanted to get a couple of things straight. My girlfriend Gloria had been asking me to take this trip with her for a couple of years. I'd always begged off, not being crazy about some of the more basic aspects of the trip. For example, the Coast part of Lost Coast implied a beach and I hated the beach. Already I could feel the sand filling my shoes as we slogged along in the too hot days toward the too cold nights.

The Lost part was also problematic. I'd spent the better part of my life worried that I really was lost, unable to navigate the material world. And I was suspicious that not feeling overtly lost was perhaps the best indicator of just how lost on me my own innards were. This bred a certain anxiety I couldn't quite shake.

I was also afraid of most animals larger than a parakeet and not all that comfortable in groups, let alone a group of strangers. Thank goodness it would only be strange women.

"For heaven's sake, Kris, they do these trips several times a year. They're professionals. Nothing's going to happen. Besides it's Solstice and a full moon, the ritual will be wonderful—how can we go wrong?" Gloria had a certain crispness to her optimism that lent authority to her arguments.

So it was with mixed emotions that I called Shelter Cove to get a motel for the night before the trip was to begin.

"Sorry honey," a woman wheezed into the phone, "motel's been shut down for a while. You'll have to try for something in Redway."

Redway was a good fifty miles inland from Shelter Cove and, according to the brochure, approximately two and one half hours by car. "So that's what, three months by llama?" I was mentally preparing for the rigors of the trip.

"Do you always have to be so negative? I could really do without the sarcastic commentary on every little detail of the trip. This is my vacation, and I'd really appreciate your keeping your nastier thoughts to yourself. I, for one, intend to enjoy myself." Gloria was looking at me over the top of *Llama World* magazine, whose cover showed a full-face close-up of a large-eyed, long-necked, small-eared, camel-lipped animal smirking directly into the camera under a caption that read Sugar and Spice and Everything Nice; How to Live With Your Llama.

"God Gloria, I'm just not sure about this. I don't want to

ruin your vacation either, but ..." My voice trailed off in an uncertainty that I couldn't conceal. "I'm really worried about the llamas, I mean I don't want to—"

Gloria cut me off. "Is that your problem? Well don't worry, I'll take care of all the llama stuff, I'm really looking forward to it."

On the late June morning that we set out for Blacksands Beach from our Redway motel I was in pretty good spirits, humming as I mentally checked and re-checked our gear from the list we'd been sent. Even with the optional underwear, we were each well within our twenty-pound weight limit. By the time we'd driven through Briceland it was obvious that the brochure must have been dated; we were going to arrive at the rendezvous point at least forty-five minutes early.

"Do you think this is the fork that looks like an upside-down wishbone?" I wasn't at all sure about our location.

"Probably. Anyway, we're so close I'm sure we can't go too far wrong," Gloria answered, looking the other way.

The road slowly became gravel before it narrowed to a single lane, winding up to a ridge that might have overlooked Shelter Cove if it hadn't been completely shrouded in fog. By the time I inched to a spot wide enough to turn us around and get back to the fork, which wasn't the upside-down wishbone, but the owl's foot—oh how could I have mistaken the two?—it was getting a bit frosty in the car.

"I suppose now we'll be late." Gloria was very punctual.

At 9:05 we bounced sharply into the gravel parking lot, and

through the coastal fog got our first glimpse of the rest of the group. Like grapes they seemed to hang out in bunches. Bunches of women. Bunches of packs. Bunches of hay. And a bunch of llamas. I felt my spirits sinking in the cold and fog.

"I'm so glad we're doing this together, isn't it great."

She had a way of tapping right into my psychic wavelength all right. I hoped my exposed teeth looked like a smile as I started toward the plastic Porta-Jane to meditate on my imminent misery. Sweaty, smelly, hairy animals. Strong, sweaty, smelly, hairy animals. Big, strong... why had I ever agreed to this? I was in imminent danger of losing it.

"Come on Kris. You can't spend all day in there."

"Okay, okay. Just a minute, I think my zipper's stuck."

"Stop it right now. Your pants don't even have a zipper. You're starting to look like a snob. Now get out here and let's get acquainted."

I opened the door to see Gloria's back heading toward one of the large vans across the lot. Gloria was one of those people who threw herself into new situations with such verve and goodwill that the contrast between us rose between my shoulder blades like a mosquito bite just out of reach.

"Are you Kris or Glorrie?"

I cringed for the pallid woman smiling from under flat burnt-madrone bangs; Glorrie indeed. "Kris. And my friend's name is Glori-a."

Who was this woman? Gauzy pants that ballooned like a circus tent in the wind, a slinky sleeveless shirt and thongs. She must have gotten her vacation brochures mixed up. But how could she know our names? I smiled my mouth-full-of-Novocain smile as she introduced herself.

"I'm Robin," she chirped, "one of the co-leaders of the trip."

Really, what was I in for? The Lost Coast Wilderness Area, impassable even to hikers at points, and here I was at the mercy of a modified belly dancer in thongs. I don't even own thongs. I put my sunglasses on as she pointed to a bulky woman in worn jeans and a battered straw hat attentively adjusting a strap under what had to be a llama. "That's Marty. My co-leader."

With her hiking boots and deep tan, Marty at least looked like she'd done this before. I smiled.

Marty waved me over, calling, "Say howdy to Pecos." I shuffled in their direction. "Give me your hand." She grabbed my arm above the elbow and used it to club Pecos, who didn't seem to register my touch as a blow. As she swept my hand down his neck and along his back I was mildly surprised at the lushness of his coat. I'd expected something more bristly, more off-putting. Perhaps these animals needn't be quite so intimidating, maybe I could learn to like them. Well, if not like them exactly, maybe I could at least not be terrified of them. Just as I was relaxing into the moment, Marty passed along a salient piece of information. "You know something weird about llamas? Their penises face backwards!"

If she'd meant to loosen me up, to draw me out, her strategy failed. I pulled back, making mental notes about personal inter-action, and re-thought my plan to bring up the rear. Looking for

Gloria, I saw her at the back of a second large van surrounded by tarps piled with everyone's little bundles of excitement and expectation. I realized that my own not so little bundle was, more than anything else, made up of wariness and trepidation. I stood staring at my shoelaces, wondering why I couldn't place my feet. I could see my boots, knew my feet had to be in them, but I could not feel them. The longer I stood there, the less I could see them; they blended and filled my field of vision before dissolving into the dust.

Slowly the group filtered toward Robin as she finished the process of weighing each piece of equipment before instructing us how to fill and then load the packs onto the llamas. This was to be one of our most time-consuming daily activities, the weighing and balancing of the loads for each animal as we consumed foodstuffs and supplies. Apparently nothing spooked or upset a llama like an unbalanced or shifting load. Determined to show both Gloria and myself that I would join in and do my part, I volunteered to help load the packs onto the llamas. It went smoothly enough, the llamas disinterestedly shrugging into the packs as we slung them across their backs. By the time I finished strapping the kitchen gear squarely onto the center of the saddle at my eye-level, I had relaxed enough to start counting, not hours or days, but women and llamas. Twelve women. Six llamas.

Robin announced that there was no need for disappointment: "You'll all have your turn leading the animals in the days ahead."

Or not, in my case.

As we started out of the parking lot, Gloria with a llama in tow, I voiced my thought that didn't she find it a little odd that our only introductions had been to the llamas and Marty and Robin.

"I suppose so, but you could make a little effort, you know. I've met almost everyone and you could have too. You still can, there's plenty of time, seven miles today alone, so stop looking for things to complain about." Gloria stopped and turned to face me directly before continuing, concern clouding her blue eyes. "Kris, this isn't going to be a lot of fun for me if you don't stop looking for what either is wrong, or could go wrong. Can you please try to relax and enjoy yourself?" She squeezed my hand and turned to head back up the beach. We fell into the silence of those who have walked long and well together, me knowing both that Gloria was right, and that I remained uneasy.

We were headed North on a narrow strip of uneven beach. To our right were hardscrabble escarpments that eroded onto the beach, which itself was not sand but palm-sized black matte stones, with a few large boulders at the stream mouths which appeared every twenty minutes or so. Some of these streams were large enough that the cliffs split to reveal endless slopes of evergreen forest swelling to fill the entire landscape, tiers of trees climbing up and up, leaving only the thinnest slice of sky at the very edge of sight. Up the gauzy ravines fog still draped in and out of the trees, a milky cloak shouldered by the Douglas fir that were so plentiful here. The coastal combination of heat and damp made for a region of not only the enormous red-woods that Northern California is so famous for, but of the smaller, more discrete varieties of pine, including the fabled Doug fir of my childhood in the Pacific Northwest.

I felt an odd sense of home that both surprised and quieted me. Not that I am used to living in a forest; rather I am used to living in the timbers from such a forest. The house that I lived in at the moment was all open beams and ceilings of rough sawn Douglas fir. So in a sense, these trees were my interior sky.

Just as they were the ground of so many childhood stories. My favorite uncle had worked for Weyerhauser Lumber and he was full of industrial grade information about various trees, but his clear favorite was the yellow pine, or Douglas fir—Oregon's state tree, "the tree that says home to any native Pacific Northwester." For my uncle Frank, if your house contained Douglas fir—and it was inconceivable that it would not—you could say your house was made of carbon dioxide, water and sunlight, that in a sense, your home was made of air. This was not a concept generally embraced in my family, but I loved Frank for his lovely willingness to talk this way.

But something else was nagging at me, something more basic to my own sense of home. And something more basic to the trees.

Douglas fir breaks easily but heals its wounds. Twenty percent to fifty percent of its mass is underground and sometimes its roots will reach out and join the roots of a cut or shattered stump. The buddy trees will keep the stump alive for hundreds of years, its top scabbing over with bark and its growth continuing. I liked that, liked the idea of buddy trees taking care of what was shattered and broken, of connections made with what remained underground. This was moving to me. I was at home with this sense of joining.

It was difficult to walk on the rocky beach; my heels hit low, digging into the pebble mash between stones, instep arching, curling, and finally rolling over the larger rocks. I was trying to get a rhythm in my walking but the unevenness of the beach made it impossible. I settled for keeping my balance. The llamas appeared to have no such problems, their tiny feet seeming to have built-in gyroscopes that kept their upper bodies both propelled and righted. They dogpaddled through the air, heads and necks stretching out and up, up and out.

By mid afternoon I was thoroughly exhausted, unused to the beach dig and stride. The seven miles that I'd been so scornful of as we started the day felt like seventy by three-thirty when we reached Gitchell Creek, our first night's camp. Marty showed us how to tether the llamas and remove the packs. We were on a large grassy flat that seemed to shrink as I looked for a place to sleep that was out of reach of the llamas.

I was relieved to see Robin standing on a scrubby strip above the flat waving to us. After hauling our gear up, we chose our sleeping spots and laid down our ground covers, still needing to gather wood, haul water, build a fire and cook dinner.

As we ate Robin informed us, "Tomorrow is a short day distance-wise, but a full day time-wise. Just past Shipman Creek there's a point that's passable only at low tide, and only at the lowest part of the low tide. It sounds simple, but it's really a tricky passage, difficult footing for the animals, and longer than it looks from this side. We'll have a leisurely lunch at Buck Creek waiting for the tide, the llamas like it there and a little ways up creek there's a waterfall that widens into a swimming hole for us. At Shipman we'll stop for a snack and re-check all the packs before actually starting around the point. Once we start we only have a half an hour to get all of us all the way around. Look at your maps and ask any questions now or sometime tomorrow before we get to Shipman. Don't wait until we're committed to the point to freak out." This last was said with an intensity that was at odds with her posture. Robin was leaning back against a rock with one arm drooping languidly on a knee, seemingly thinking about nothing more urgent than where her next doobie was coming from.

As some of us pulled out our maps, she continued, "Past Shipman it's easy terrain up to Big Flat, our layover camp. There's a beach where we usually build a sweathouse. You can hike up Big Flat Creek or just hang out—whatever you're up for."

At the moment I wasn't up for anything more than sitting around the fire in the suddenly swarming fog. What had been a high haze an hour ago was now a damp gauze that completely obscured the rising moon. Even without a sea breeze, the chill got under my T-shirt and wrapped itself around my ribs like a frigid Ace bandage. Introductions were started while I dug around in my pack for an over-shirt.

Of the twelve of us, Gloria and I were the only couple, though seven of the women knew someone or had taken one of these trips before, so there were only three true solitaires among us. Of these, Deborah was the least likeable to me. Small and wiry, with long black hair gathered loosely at her neck and an expression pulled tight behind dark sunglasses that sat low on her nose, she referred to herself as a biker babe. She was at once in your face and hidden. I was fairly sure that the stones on the beach had more give in them than she did. Since my own brittleness was longer-limbed, I considered myself more evolved and hoped not to have too much to do with the Divine Mrs. D. Not everybody felt compelled to say anything very personal, which was a relief to me, since I hated knowing too much of what a person said before knowing how they did. One of the most appealing things about a group of strangers was just that—you could be as strange as you wanted to be. Being a stranger to your daily life was one way to try on new ideas. Gloria really hated this kind of thinking, but I cherished the chance to be someone else for a few days.

Gloria had spent most of the late afternoon walking with Bettina, a German woman who made jewelry in San Francisco. As I looked across the fire at them, they seemed of a piece; both were tall and open-faced with shoulder-length hair so curly it stayed pretty much in place despite the wind. I was glad for

Gloria to find someone she liked so easily. We were in a cramped place in our relationship, and one of the reasons we'd wanted to take this trip was to leave our dailiness behind, to enjoy new people and experiences without having to hang on to each other quite so tightly as we seemed to do at home.

That night I woke several times to unfamiliar sounds. Once, positive that a wolf was methodically stalking me, I clutched at Gloria's bag while cautioning, "Shhh! Something's out there, I've been awake for hours and it's almost on top of us now."

A long silence, then, "I don't believe this. Would you leave me alone. There's nothing to be afraid of. It's probably just a rabbit. Besides, if it were anything dangerous the llamas would be carrying on." She turned her back to me with a parting thought. "You could drive a person crazy, you know that?"

Unconvinced by her argument, I lay wide awake, unsure whether my abject terror or my urgent need to pee was making me most miserable.

"I. Am. So. Mad. At. You." Each word surprisingly distinct in the heavy ocean air. "Now I can't sleep either."

Ignoring the venom in her voice, I whispered, "Then you do hear it, what should we do?"

"We shouldn't do anything. We should be asleep. But thanks to you that's not possible."

I could hear her fumbling around in her bag. A click. "There. Satisfied?" Illuminated in the beam of her flashlight was a vicious baby deer nibbling the bushes about ten feet from our bags.

The next morning tales of my bravery entertained everyone as we packed up. I laughed with the good-natured ribbing, but was glad to get going. I was definitely ready for things to move along.

Gloria asked if I wanted to walk with her and Bettina, but I declined, more wanting to drift along in my head, watching the flat pewter sea widening and blurring under the heavy morning fog. I'd always thought of the sea and shore as separate, related only by proximity, but looking now I couldn't tell where they became themselves, exactly. Elizabeth Bishop came to me:

> "Or does the land lean down to lift the sea
>     from under,
> drawing it unperturbed around itself?
> Along the fine tan sandy shelf
> Is the land tugging at the sea from under?"

Where was the land for my sea? Watching the sea rise and fall, the long slow swelling and release, I knew the movement intimately, internally. I also knew that what happened at the shore was not so clear to me. The choppy wash that crept away from itself, toward the land and trees, was almost unrelated to the subtle breath out near the horizon line. Perhaps I was asking the wrong question. Maybe I had too much land for my sea. How, I wondered, did the kelp both anchor and float?

My thoughts were interrupted by someone asking about lunch.

"We met in the parking lot, remember? I'm Ruthe." I hadn't remembered her name, but her outfit was unforgettable. She was wearing a white and red Japanese print scarf Bedouin-style over her head, covering the back of her neck, and faded dark blue T-shirt with a torn out neck, baggy black, green and brown splotched night-camo pants, with a navy blue sweater tied around her waist.

"Ruthe, what in hell are those things on your feet?"

"I'm not sure if they have a proper name." She laughed as we flopped down against a huge log. "I got them on sale at a martial arts store. Aren't they great?"

I'm a shoe girl, and had to admire even what I couldn't imagine wearing. "Well, they look very terrain specific, I'll give you that."

'They' were tabbies with carbuncular rubber soles, mid-calf blue-black cotton duck uppers and a sophisticated, half-hidden clip fastening system which extended up the entire length of the backside. The overall effect was of a guerilla elf on maneuvers.

Ruthe was easily fifty or so, about five foot-two, slight of build, with the oddly translucent skin of a candled egg. She owned several acres in "The Gulch," which she'd acquired through persistent and shrewd bargaining with the Bureau of Land Management. She lived in a tent at the moment, but was planning a small house, a well, and a sophisticated irrigation system. All of which she would build herself with help from friends, many of whom were on this trip.

"And I just got back from three months on a coffee brigade

working the harvest in Nicaragua. I thought it would be invaluable experience for working my own land."

I spared her my thoughts.

"So what's 'The Gulch'?" I asked, faintly annoyed at the assumption that it was the center of everyone's universe.

Ruthe looked at me as if I'd left something behind. "Whale Gulch. It's just outside of Whitethorn on the Usal Road, not far from the trailhead." She'd added this last as a desperate attempt to communicate with what must have looked like a very primitive life form to her.

I thought back to the steep forested land anywhere near the trailhead. "Jeez Ruthe I'm no farmer, but the whole idea seems impossible to me."

"Yeah, well we all do minimal impact farming. If you're willing to farm on the land's terms you can make it all right."

Oh. Right. While I understood what she was saying, I realized that I hadn't a clue as to what she meant. And as she didn't seem inclined to volunteer anymore, we ate along in silence, looking out to sea.

I set my sandwich aside, shocked at how sleepy I'd become. "It's the haze," Ruthe smiled, "it always gets me too."

I drifted into a half sleep thinking how different my life was from Ruthe's. I was the least agricultural or rural person I knew. My work put me in the heart of the kind of life that the Gulchers actively hated. I did electrical work on every kind of vehicle around—cars, trucks, commercial fishing boats, construction rigs, even police cars. I somehow felt it wise to keep that last to myself. Lots of my friends had joined the hippie back-to-the-land movement, but none had lasted. It was hard to survive this way, and harder still to actually live. These were crafty and capable women whose daily lives were unimaginable to me.

I was working on some version of underwater subsistence farming as I fell asleep. I sank into an inky pool teeming with hollow fish, phosphorescent skeletal lanterns lighting my path. Down and down. An alluvial waterscape that both compelled and frightened me. Its density held everything in place, motionless. There was simply the prescience of shape, rhythm of place. The eye in the palm of the hand.

I struggled to orient myself as we started out again. I couldn't shake the dark torpor of the dream, my entire body cold, and achingly heavy. As we moved up the beach, I was in the rear with a woman named Kathy and her llama, Whitney. We walked, me only semi-present and not very talkative. She didn't seem to mind my mood and continued to point out the occasional interesting bird sightings as if I were really there. I had noticed her yesterday, chosen her as one of the women I wanted to meet. She was a couple of inches taller than me, probably five foot nine or so and maybe forty pounds heavier and so completely self-centered that she was a study in balance and harmonics. She never appeared to change stride even in the most uneven terrain, she had an inner axis that was mobile but true. Some of the old motors I worked on had self-centering bearings. Kathy was the first person I'd seen with self-centering bearing.

We recognized something in each other, as if we might have known one another from someplace else. Like recognizing sageness in varieties of sage, we finally recognized trades-womanness in varieties of woman. I understood a patience, a quality of time out of time in Kathy that was a large portion of my daily work on vehicular electrical systems. Turns out that though she now did carpentry for a living, she'd owned her own commercial fishing boat for a few years. So what we knew about each other was more fundamental than if we'd been blood relatives; we knew how the other one worked.

She had Whitney this afternoon. Whitney, she informed me, was new to packing. This was only his second trip, and he was still fairly excitable. He wasn't used to leading and wasn't very good at following. Sounded more human by the second. His neck bobbed and dipped like he was balancing an apple on his head as he hunkered along.

As we came within sight of Buck Creek, she suddenly thrust Whitney's lead into my hand, bent and shot her hand into the receding surf to snag an enormous King salmon. I knew that because I had caught a fish very similar to this from a rowboat on Neah Bay when I was eight years old. Well, I'd hooked it and made my mother catch it, but I'd always considered it my catch.

Kathy held it up by one pink gill and announced it as a full-moon gift from the goddess.

Oh please. And I actually liked Kathy.

As everyone clambered around, squealing with delight, I considered just turning my little boat for home. I wasn't sure I could take three more days of woo-woo. Why was it better to think this was some mysterious blessing on the trip rather than to cop to arranging to have the fish waiting for us? I voiced my opinion that a perfectly healthy, if dead, salmon, just the right size to feed the entire group was very unlikely to meander ashore all by its lonesome just for us. I also pointed out the absence of any boats, fishing or otherwise anywhere in sight.

I could feel the hostility of the group as I spoke. It was Robin who finally answered. "Kris, it is much more unlikely that anyone would go to all the trouble to hike up to here with a thirty-pound salmon just to trick the group—that would be so spiritually un-cool that no one would take the risk."

Oh that explained it. "Well, I guess I've just been in the city a little too long."

Robin let it go with a big smile and agreed that things were very different here. The group visibly relaxed. Thongs or no, she had some people skills that I was momentarily grateful for.

Marty spoke up to remind us that we needed to get ourselves in gear, the tide was changing, and we had a Point to make. Kathy took off her shirt, soaked it and wrapped it around the fish. I helped her string a rope through its gills, put it in a plastic sack, and hang it on Whitney's pack. We were off.

Minutes later Whitney jerked his shoulders, screeched and spun around and around, dervish-like, throwing Kathy up into the air and down again and again as she clung desperately to his lead rope. Like ripples around a rock in a pond, we all moved away from them. Ahead of me a woman screamed and went down, clutching her right leg, which lay twisted on the rocks. At that moment Whitney broke free, turned and ran for home. Kathy took off after him.

Suddenly, no one moved but everyone was in motion. The llamas were wheezing and braying, heads swiveling, bodies rocking, ready to bolt. Before I could begin to figure out what to do, Robin got them all tethered together and facing away from the receding Whitney. She told us to keep talking to them and headed off after Kathy and Whitney.

Meanwhile, Marty was kneeling next to the downed woman, who turned out to be my favorite biker gal. They were surrounded by four or five of the others, including Gloria, in the ankle-deep tidal wash, trying to decide on the best course of action. Finally, they picked Deborah up and moved her out of the water's reach. It was clear from the expression on her face that we were going to be staying put for a while.

In all the commotion, the fish had flown off Whitney and lay forgotten in the sand. I grabbed the sack and knelt a few feet away from Marty and Deborah and the gang, close enough to hear what was going on, but not quite close enough to be part of the conversation. It was amazing to me that I still knew exactly how to clean a fish—it had been at least thirty years since I'd last done it—but my hands thought for me, I just had to follow them along. I didn't like it any better now than

I had as a youngster, but as no one else was jumping at the opportunity I carried on.

Ripples of fear and dissension had by this time made their way from the larger group to me. I sat assessing my own state. My fear was that we would be physically unable to deal with any worsening of Deborah's condition. The extra effort of carrying my ten-pound daypack made it clear that none of us was going to carry Deborah around the point, and a llama-powered litter seemed impossible for the boulders if nothing else. I looked back down the beach in hopes of seeing Kathy and Robin. No such luck.

In addition to being afraid I was angry. Angry that we'd had the accident at all, angry at the extra work I imagined if things got worse, which was all I could imagine. I was definitely losing my sense of humor. In fact this was turning into quite a trip of lost and found. My sense of humor lost, I found myself being drawn into a situation I hadn't counted on and didn't want.

Marty came over with the news. "It looks like she may be all right, but she can't walk on it yet. She wants to sit for a bit, so we may as well wait here through the next tide change and see if Robin and Kathy make it back, and then reassess the situation."

At least she sounded lucid. "Sounds good to me. I have to say that I'm not so comfortable with Deborah's decision-making capacity at the moment." I might as well get it out in the open.

"Right, but I'm a nurse and I'm comfortable with my

decision-making capacity. At the moment." Marty skewered me with her eyes, daring me to push harder.

I nodded and ignored the challenge. "Good, that makes me more comfortable all the way around." And it did. I hoped the modifier didn't stand too tall between us.

I looked at my watch and wondered if we were safe from the encroaching tide. After all, the whole point of breaking up the day this way had been to coordinate with the tide. I thought we should go back to Buck—it was so close and relatively comfortable. It was sheltered, and a good spot to get an evacuation unit into if necessary.

"We have a portable CB," Marty said. "So it isn't like we're stranded. And this strip is wide enough to stay as long as we need to. I think we should just wait until the others get back. The longer Deborah's quiet, the better."

I knew the end of a discussion when I heard it. So we waited—actually I wished I could just wait, but I noticed myself start to wait—a very different proposition indeed. I felt like I was on the clock for no particularly good reason and with no end in sight.

I caught Gloria's eye and motioned her over. "Just want you to know I'm not ignoring you." I smiled as I spoke.

"Oh, I know—it's really okay isn't it." This wasn't said as a question, it was more like the sharing of a recent rare bird sighting.

"Yeah. Maybe we need to be strangerly together more often. Anyway, you heard what I said, and I know you don't entirely agree, and . . . well . . . I'm glad for you to have a friend and some company. I'm keenly aware that I'm not Ms. Nice-Nice here, and I just hope it doesn't rub off on you."

"Sweet. But don't worry. Nobody hates you—they all think you're kind of a curmudgeon, but a cute curmudgeon. Benefit of the doubt—after all, you are with me." With that, Gloria kissed the top of my head and headed back to the nurses' station.

Yeah, that was me, sweet but . . . Somebody yelled, and I looked down the beach to see Kathy and Robin, Whitney in tow, not too far away. I checked at my watch. Three-thirty. Well, technically, there was still one more chance at 6:40 or so to make it past Shipman before the tide and the light were against us. But none of us seemed quite technical enough to make me want to try it. I could only hope that sanity prevailed.

Deborah thought she could make it to Shipman on her own feet with someone's help. Robin deferred to Marty. Kathy tended to my way of thinking, wondering if Deborah was really able to assess her own situation. Ruthe just accepted Deborah as whole in her present condition—for Ruthe it was as if Deborah had never been unhurt. In Ruthe's view Deborah's injury had no effect whatever on her presence of mind. The others were the young and enthusiastic to whom extra work was just some more fun and disaster a foreign concept. So it was decided that we'd go to Shipman, and that Raven, Robin's niece's girlfriend, would be Deborah's third leg. I volunteered to carry Raven's pack, and Bettina took Deborah's.

We started out again, Robin leading Whitney, the fish safely on an older, more veteran animal, the rest of us strung out loosely behind them, Raven and Deborah bringing up the rear. Deborah's knee was swollen to the size of a volleyball, and she was in so much pain that she was already nauseous and hollow-eyed. She could put no weight on the leg, and we still had forty-five minutes to the point if she were walking normally. No telling how long hopping.

At Shipman, we waited more than an hour for Raven and Deborah. Marty had done the math and figured we could still make it. I thought it was nuts. "I hope the fear of ruining twelve vacations isn't figuring in this decision?" I was as sympathetic as anyone to the financial impact of turning back, but this just seemed crazy. "You've said the beach around the point is, and I quote, 'viciously difficult,' in the best of times, and these, clearly, are not the best of times."

Everyone just looked at me. Maybe, just maybe, I was getting through.

"She's going to have to ride one of the llamas." Kathy said it while turning to Robin who was already checking pack weights in her notebook.

"Right. I want her on Pecos—he's an old hand and I'll lead him myself."

I felt my innards shift with this exchange—I knew it was fruitless to give voice to any more concerns. We were going on and I needed to decide for myself whether I was going too. I knew Gloria was comfortable with the group and wanted to go on. Myself, I'd always found issues of staying and going entirely too confusing. I looked out at the late-afternoon swells—the sea is always more active in the afternoon—and watched the sets rolling by, aware that I didn't really know how to leave her, not exactly news to me.

I stared at the surf nibbling hare-lipped at the pebbles. If I was in this for the duration I might as well be useful. "I can take a little more weight—there's some room in my pack."

It was 5:30, we still had a good three-plus hours of daylight, and if we got going at 6:05, the tide was with us.

Deborah's face contorted with pain as she was lifted and tied onto Pecos. Llama saddles are not made for sitting, so even if you weren't injured it would be a rough ride, but in Deborah's condition it was obviously at the outer limit of endurable as Pecos jerked and jagged over the rocks. It was here, dealing in extremis, that I finally saw Robin, understood why all these folks thought she was so special. She loved these llamas, they weren't just some gimmicky way to wrest a living out of city folk, much as I had wanted to see it that way. Her ability to keep Pecos focused on the immediate next step instead of his passenger was more miraculous to me than the fish. She never stopped talking to him, telling him what was next, how well he was doing, how she knew it was hard for him, and how much she needed and relied on him. She talked to him in a voice I'd not heard, a voice that hinted at the difficulty of the decision to go forward, a voice completely devoid of the tinny falsetto that I now realized had signaled an otherwise unacknowledged danger to me. But this voice was so warm and rich that I knew it to be her inner voice, perhaps her lover's voice, for surely Pecos was attendant and attuned to her the way lovers sometimes are.

Keeping my own feet took such concentration that I had no sense of landscape apart from what was precisely underfoot. I don't recall being individually aware of anyone else, yet I had a caterpillared sense of our movement, each person coupled to the next by a tension which obliterated any sense of linear time as we inched over the rocky littoral. It was only when my steps became awkwardly un-landed that I realized we were on the coastal version of dirt—an acridly aromatic mix of sand, grasses and evergreen needles. We trudged past the rocks and started up the trail to the headlands and on to Big Flat. Which was a perfect description of my state. I was so big-flat that all I wanted to do was throw myself on the ground and weep. There was, however, water to get, llamas to unload and tether, a fire to make and a meal to cook. Not to mention an invalid to care for.

Had I been alone I would not have gotten the water. I would not have built a fire. I would not have eaten. I would have crawled into my sleeping bag and felt sorry for myself. Gloriously, fluorescently sorry for myself. Sadly I was not alone. Not alone, and not willing to expose the extent of my fatigue to this particular gang. I had a coward's sense of vulnerability; I had not yet learned that there are many types of exposure, nearly none fatal.

Gloria, Bettina and I drew the water detail. We each took a five-gallon canvas bucket and followed Robin's directions to the stream. On the way we found a tree limb to lay over our shoulders. We staggered back to camp single file, strung along the pole, water, human, water, human, water, human. I was the last human, and the hardest to distinguish as such, so sloppy wet was I, having managed to overfill and then nearly empty my bucket as I stumbled my way along. We returned to both a large campfire and a smaller cookfire and a surprisingly quiet feeling of general goodwill.

I volunteered to cook the fish both in order to steam myself dry and because I can't bear to eat fish—especially not one I've cleaned. Only Gloria knew that I wouldn't eat the salmon, and she said nothing—for which I was inordinately grateful.

In my world, sharing a meal is as close to ritual as I get, and I surely wasn't up to yet another overt display of my Philistine tendencies. And in my own way, I did share this meal. I found myself loving the cooking amidst the combination of smoke, wispy fog fingering its way inland and fading light. In the distance I could hear the long slow belly-breath of the sea overlaid with what sounded like the barking of sea lions, and closer, the occasional owl or owls called back and forth. And though the moon had not yet risen, the stars were slowly lighting up the darkening sky, providing me with all the company I could want, just at that moment.

I thought about the day, the difficulty and the beauty of it. The whole crazy notion of me being here at all. But it wasn't wholly crazy; I did love the coast, I did love being so away from my daily life, and I certainly did know how to carry a pack and make a camp. And then there was the utterly simple opening to myself, to my own heart, my own hearth, to the fire that I keep so banked back inside myself. That opening was the real reason for my discomfort—I always want to open in private. It was that question of exposure again. It was much easier for me to have certain knowledge or opinionated purpose than to sit still in public. In an odd way, the difficulties and terrors of the day suited my public self just fine—the smoke screen of "what we should have done" allowed me to hide in my superior self.

How precious.

I looked over to the campfire and the women gathered around it. While it was not my time to join them, it was time for me to join myself, to stand in this gutted light and be still.

As I sit in my sunroom on this darkest day of the year, another Solstice more than twenty years away from the events I've just related, I'm no nearer understanding their hold on me. I've often thought about what happened on that trip. I am still gripped by the trip yet not at all engaged with "what happened." It was a turning point in my life in many ways, and the actual events are not the issue; it is my own grappling with the way the memories and memory itself have worked in me that remains.

I know almost nothing of the subsequent lives of the women from that trip, though I do know that Deborah was rescued the second day from Big Flat and taken by all-terrain vehicle back to civilization. From there I have no idea of her fate.

My former lover and I are close, though from opposite sides of the continent. So it remains edgy for me, this trip. We talked a bit about it the last time she was in town and agreed that the experience was almost impossible to relate to others. Though we didn't sort out why that might be, I've come to believe it is because the descriptions of the events don't carry the complexity of memory. That is, what occurred is not what happened.

If the original meaning of Solstice is the time that the sun stands still, perhaps it is time for me to honor just standing with the beauty of not knowing. And accept the gift that the willingness to simply be still is.

# A TRADITIONAL CHRISTMAS

## Val McDermid

Last night, I dreamed I went to Amberley. Snow had fallen, deep and crisp and even, garlanding the trees like tinsel sparkling in the sunlight as we swept through the tall iron gates and up the drive. Diana was driving, her gloved hands assured on the wheel in spite of the hazards of an imperfectly cleared surface. We rounded the coppice, and there was the house, perfect as a photograph, the sun seeming to breathe life into the golden Cotswold stone. Amberley House, one of the little jobs Vanbrugh knocked off once he'd learned the trade with Blenheim Palace.

Diana stopped in front of the portico and blared the horn. She turned to me, eyes twinkling, smile bewitching as ever. "Christmas begins here," she said. As if on cue, the front door opened and Edmund stood framed in the doorway, flanked by his and Diana's mother, and his wife Jane, all smiling as gaily as daytrippers.

I woke then, rigid with shock, pop-eyed in the dark. It was one of those dreams so vivid that when you waken, you can't quite believe it has just happened. But I knew it was a dream. A nightmare, rather. For Edmund, sixth Baron Amberley of Anglezarke, had been dead for three months. I should know. I found the body.

Beside me, Diana was still asleep. I wanted to burrow into her side, seeking comfort from the horrors of memory, but I couldn't bring myself to be so selfish. A proper night's sleep was still a luxury for her and the next couple of weeks weren't exactly going to be restful. I slipped out of bed and went through to the kitchen to make a cup of camomile tea.

I huddled over the gas fire and forced myself to think back to Christmas. It was the fourth year that Diana and I had made the trip back to her ancestral home to celebrate. As our first Christmas together had approached, I'd worried about what we were going to do. In relationships like ours, there isn't a standard formula. The only thing I was sure about was that I wanted us to spend it together. I knew that meant visiting my parents was out. As long as they never have to confront the physical evidence of my lesbianism, they can handle it. Bringing any woman home to their tenement flat in Glasgow for Christmas would be uncomfortable. Bringing the daughter of a baron would be impossible.

When I'd nervously broached the subject, Diana had looked

astonished, her eyebrows raised, her mouth twitching in a half-smile. "I assumed you'd want to come to Amberley with me," she said. "They're expecting you to."

"Are you sure?"

Diana grabbed me in a bear-hug. "Of course I'm sure. Don't you want to spend Christmas with me?"

"Stupid question," I grunted. "I thought maybe we could celebrate on our own, just the two of us. Romantic, intimate, that sort of thing."

Diana looked uncertain. "Can't we be romantic at Amberley? I can't imagine Christmas anywhere else. It's so . . . traditional. So English."

My turn for the raised eyebrows. "Sure I'll fit in?"

"You know my mother thinks the world of you. She insists on you coming. She's fanatical about tradition, especially Christmas. You'll love it," she promised.

And I did. Unlikely as it is, this Scottish working-class lesbian feminist homeopath fell head over heels for the whole English country-house package. I loved driving down with Diana on Christmas Eve, leaving the motorway traffic behind, slipping through narrow lanes with their tall hedgerows, driving through the chocolate-box village of Amberley, fairy lights strung round the green, and, finally, cruising past the Dower House where her mother lived and on up the drive. I loved the sherry and mince pies with the neighbours, even the ones who wanted to regale me with their ailments. I loved the elaborate Christmas Eve meal Diana's mother cooked. I loved the brisk walk through the woods to the village church for the midnight service. I loved most of all the way they simply absorbed me into their ritual without distance.

Christmas Day was champagne breakfast, stockings crammed with childish toys and expensive goodies from the Sloane Ranger shops, church again, then presents proper. The gargantuan feast of Christmas dinner, with free-range turkey from the estate's home farm. Then a dozen close family friends arrived to pull crackers, wear silly hats and masks, drink like tomorrow was another life and play every ridiculous party game from Sardines to Charades. I'm glad no one's ever videotaped the evening and threatened to send a copy to the women's alternative health co-operative where I practise. I'd have to pay the blackmail. Diana and I lead a classless life in London, where almost no one knows her background. It's not that she's embarrassed. It's just that she knows from bitter experience how many barriers it builds for her. But at Amberley, we left behind my homeopathy and her Legal Aid practice, and for a few days we lived in a time warp that Charles Dickens would have revelled in.

On Boxing Day night, we always trooped down to the village hall for the dance. It was then that Edmund came into his own. His huntin', shootin' and fishin' persona slipped from him like the masks we'd worn the night before when he picked up his alto sax and stepped onto the stage to lead the twelve-piece Amber Band. Most of his fellow members were professional session musicians, but the drummer doubled as a labourer on Amberley Farm and the keyboard player was the village postman. I'm no connoisseur, but I reckoned the Amber Band was one of the best live outfits I've ever heard. They played everything from Duke Ellington to Glenn Miller, including Miles Davis and John Coltrane pieces, all arranged by Edmund. And of course, they played some of Edmund's own compositions, strange haunting slow-dancing pieces that somehow achieved the seemingly impossible marriage between the English countryside and jazz.

There was nothing different to mark out last Christmas as a watershed gig. Edmund led the band with his usual verve. Diana and I danced with each other half the night and took it in turns to dance with her mother the rest of the time. Evangeline ("call me Evie") still danced with a vivacity and flair that made me understand why Diana's father had fallen for her. As usual, Jane sat stolidly nursing a gin and tonic that she made last the whole night. "I don't dance," she'd said stiffly to me when I'd asked her up on my first visit. It was a rebuff that brooked no argument. Later, I asked Diana if Jane had knocked me back because I was a dyke.

Diana roared with laughter. "Good God, no," she spluttered. "Jane doesn't even dance with Edmund. She's tone deaf and has no sense of rhythm."

"Bit of a handicap, being married to Edmund," I said.

Diana shrugged. "It would be if music were the only thing he did. But the Amber Band only does a few gigs a year. The rest of the time he's running the estate and Jane loves being the country squire's wife."

In the intervening years, that was the only thing that had changed. Word of mouth had increased the demand for the Amber Band's services. By last Christmas, the band were playing at least one gig a week. They'd moved up from playing village halls and hunt balls onto the student-union circuit.

Last Christmas I'd gone for a walk with Diana's mother on the afternoon of Christmas Eve. As we'd emerged from the back door, I noticed a three-ton van parked over by the stables. Along the side, in tall letters of gold and black, it said, "Amber Band! Bringing jazz to the people."

"Wow," I said, "That looks serious."

Evie laughed. "It keeps Edmund happy. His father was obsessed with breaking the British record for the largest salmon, which, believe me, was a far more inconvenient interest than Edmund's. All Jane has to put up with is a lack of Edmund's company two or three nights a week at most. Going alone to a dinner party is a far lighter cross to bear than being dragged off to fishing lodges in the middle of nowhere to be bitten to death by midges."

"Doesn't he find it hard, trying to run the estate as well?" I asked idly as we struck out across the park towards the coppice.

Evie's lips pursed momentarily, but her voice betrayed no irritation. "He's taken a man on part-time to take care of the day-to-day business. Edmund keeps his hands firmly on the reins, but Lewis has taken on the burden of much of the routine work."

"It can't be easy, making an estate like this pay nowadays."

Evie smiled. "Edmund's very good at it. He understands the importance of tradition, but he's not afraid to try new things. I'm very lucky with my children, Jo. They've turned out better than any mother could have hoped."

I accepted the implied compliment in silence.

The happy family idyll crashed around everyone's ears the day after Boxing Day. Edmund had seemed quieter than usual over lunch, but I put that down to the hangover that, if there were any justice in the world, he should be suffering. As Evie poured out the coffee, he cleared his throat and said abruptly, "I've got something to say to you all."

Diana and I exchanged questioning looks. I noticed Jane's face freeze, her fingers clutching the handle of her coffee cup. Evie finished what she was doing and sat down. "We're all listening, Edmund," she said gently.

"As you're all aware, Amber Band has become increasingly successful. A few weeks ago, I was approached by a representative of a major record company. They would like us to sign a deal with them to make some recordings. They would also like to help us move our touring venues up a gear or two. I've discussed this with the band, and we're all agreed that we would be crazy to turn our backs on this opportunity." Edmund paused and looked around apprehensively.

"Congratulations, bro," Diana said. I could hear the nervousness in her voice, though I wasn't sure why she was so apprehensive. I sat silent, waiting for the other shoe to drop.

"Go on," Evie said in a voice so unemotional it sent a chill to my heart.

"Obviously, this is something that has implications for Amberley. I can't have a career as a musician and continue to be responsible for all of this. Also, we need to increase the income from the estate in order to make sure that whatever happens to my career, there will always be enough money available to allow Ma to carry on as she has always done. So I have made the decision to hand over the running of the house and the estate to a management company who will run the house as a residential conference centre and manage the land in broad accordance with the principles I've already established," Edmund said in a rush.

Jane's face flushed dark red. "How dare you?" she hissed. "You can't turn this place into some bloody talking shop. The house will be full of ghastly sales reps. Our lives won't be our own."

Edmund looked down at the table. "We won't be here," he said softly. "It makes more sense if we move out. I thought we could take a house in London." He looked up beseechingly at Jane, a look so naked it was embarrassing to witness it.

"This is extraordinary," Evie said, finding her voice at last. "Hundreds of years of tradition, and you want to smash it to pieces to indulge some hobby?"

Edmund took a deep breath. "Ma, it's not a hobby. It's the only time I feel properly alive. Look, this is not a matter for discussion. I've made my mind up. The house and the estate are mine absolutely to do with as I see fit, and these are my plans. There's no point in argument. The papers are all drawn up and I'm going to town tomorrow to sign them. The other chaps from the village have already handed in their notice. We're all set."

Jane stood up. "You bastard," she yelled. "You inconsiderate bastard! Why didn't you discuss this with me?"

Edmund raised his hands out to her. "I knew you'd be opposed to it. And you know how hard I find it to say no to you. Jane, I need to do this. It'll be fine, I promise you. We'll find somewhere lovely to live in London, near your friends."

Wordlessly, Jane picked up her coffee cup and hurled it at Edmund. It caught him in the middle of the forehead. He barely flinched as the hot liquid poured down his face, turning his sweater brown. "You insensitive pig," she said in a low voice. "Hadn't you noticed I haven't had a period for two months? I'm pregnant, Edmund, you utter bastard. I'm two months' pregnant and you want to turn my life upside down?" Then she ran from the room, slamming the heavy door behind her, no mean feat in itself.

In the stunned silence that followed Jane's bombshell, no one moved. Then Edmund, his face seeming to disintegrate, pushed his chair back with a screech and hurried wordlessly after his wife. I turned to look at Diana. The sight of her stricken face was like a blow to the chest. I barely registered Evie sighing, "How sharper than a serpent's tooth," before she too left the room. Before the door closed behind her, I was out of my chair, Diana pressed close to me.

Dinner that evening was the first meal I'd eaten at Amberley in an atmosphere of strain. Hardly a word was spoken, and I suspect I wasn't alone in feeling relief when Edmund rose abruptly before coffee and announced he was going down to the village to rehearse. "Don't wait up," he said tersely.

Jane went upstairs as soon as the meal was over. Evie sat down with us to watch a film, but half an hour into it, she rose and said, "I'm sorry. I'm not concentrating. Your brother has given me rather too much to think about. I'm going back to the Dower House."

Diana and I walked to the door with her mother. We stood under the portico, watching the dark figure against the snow. The air was heavy, the sky lowering. "Feels like a storm brewing," Diana remarked. "Even the weather's cross with Edmund."

We watched the rest of the film then decided to go up to bed. As we walked through the hall, I went to switch off the lights on the Christmas tree. "Leave them," Diana said. "Edmund will turn them off when he comes in. It's tradition—last to bed does the tree." She smiled reminiscently. "The number of times I've come back from parties in the early hours and seen the tree shining down the drive."

About an hour later, the storm broke. We were reading in bed when a clap of thunder as loud as a bomb blast crashed over the house. Then a rattle of machine-gun fire against the window. We clutched each other in surprise, though heaven knows we've never needed an excuse. Diana slipped out of bed and pulled back one of the heavy damask curtains so we could watch the hail pelt the window and the bolts of lightning flash jagged across the sky. It raged for nearly half an hour. Diana and I played the game of counting the gap between thunder-claps and lightning flashes, which told us the storm seemed to be circling Amberley itself, moving off only to come back and blast us again with lightning and hail.

Eventually it moved off to the west, occasional flashes lighting up the distant hills. Somehow, it seemed the right time to make love. As we lay together afterwards, revelling in the luxury of satiated sensuality, the lights suddenly went out. "Damn," Diana drawled. "Bloody storm's got the electrics on the blink." She stirred. "I'd better go down and check the fuse box."

I grabbed her. "Leave it," I urged. "Edmund can do it when he comes in. We're all warm and sleepy. Besides, I might get lonely."

Diana chuckled and snuggled back into my arms. Moments later, the lights came back on again. "See?" I said. "No need. Probably a problem at the local sub-station because of the weather."

❖ ❖ ❖

I woke up just after seven the following morning, full of the joys of spring. We were due to go back to London after lunch, so I decided to sneak out for an early-morning walk in the copse. I dressed without waking Diana and slipped out of the silent house.

The path from the house to the copse was well-trodden. There had been no fresh snow since Christmas Eve, and the path was well used, since it was a short cut both to the Dower House and the village. There were even mountain-bike tracks among the scattered boot prints. The trees, an elderly mixture of beech, birch, alder, oak and ash, still held their tracery of snow on the tops of some branches, though following the storm a mild thaw had set in. As I moved into the wood, I felt drips of melting snow on my head.

In the middle of the copse, there's a clearing fringed with silver birch trees. When she was little, Diana was convinced this was the place where the fairies came to recharge their magic. There was no magic in the clearing that morning. As soon as I emerged from the trees, I saw Edmund's body, sprawled under a single silver birch tree by the path on the far side.

For a moment, I was frozen with shock. Then I rushed forward and crouched down beside him. I didn't need to feel for a pulse. He was clearly long dead, his right hand blackened and burned.

I can't remember the next hours. Apparently, I went to the Dower House and roused Evie. I blurted out what I'd seen and she called the police. I have a vague recollection of her staggering slightly as I broke the news, but I was in shock and I have no recollection of what she said. Diana arrived soon afterwards. When her mother told her what had happened, she stared numbly at me for a moment, then tears poured down her face. None of us seemed eager to be the one to break the news to Jane. Eventually, as if by mutual consent, we waited until the police arrived. We merited two uniformed constables, plus two plain-clothes detectives. In the words of Noël Coward, Detective Inspector Maggie Staniforth would not have fooled a drunken child of two and a half. As soon as Evie introduced me as her daughter's partner, DI Staniforth thawed visibly. I didn't much care at that point. I was too numbed even to take in what they were saying. It sounded like the distant mutter of bees in a herb garden.

DI Staniforth set off with her team to examine the body while Diana and I, after a muttered discussion in the corner, informed Evie that we would go and tell Jane. We found her in the kitchen drinking a mug of coffee. "I don't suppose you've seen my husband," she said in tones of utter contempt when we walked in. "He didn't have the courage to come home last night."

Diana sat down next to Jane and flashed me a look of panic. I stepped forward. "I'm sorry, Jane, but there's been an accident." In moments of crisis, why is it we always reach for the nearest cliché?

Jane looked at me as if I were speaking Swahili. "An

accident?" she asked in a macabre echo of Dame Edith Evans's "A handbag?"

"Edmund's dead," Diana blurted out. "He was struck by lightning in the wood. Coming home from the village."

As she spoke, a wave of nausea surged through me. I thought I was going to faint. I grabbed the edge of the table. Diana's words robbed the muscles in my legs of their strength and I lurched into the nearest chair. Up until that point, I'd been too dazed with shock to realize the conclusion everyone but me had come to.

Jane looked blankly at Diana. "I'm so sorry," Diana said, the tears starting again, flowing down her cheeks.

"I'm not," Jane said. "He can't stop my child growing up in Amberley now."

Diana turned white. "You bitch," she said wonderingly.

At least I knew then what I had to do.

Maggie Staniforth arrived shortly after to interview me. "It's just a formality," she said. "It's obvious what happened. He was walking home in the storm and was struck by lightning as he passed under the birch tree."

I took a deep breath. "I'm afraid not," I said. "Edmund was murdered."

Her eyebrows rose. "You're still in shock. I'm afraid there are no suspicious circumstances."

"Maybe not to you. But I know different."

Credit where it's due, she heard me out. But the sceptical look never left her eyes. "That's all very well," she said eventually.

"But if what you're saying is true, there's no way of proving it."

I shrugged. "Why don't you look for fingerprints? Either in the plug of the Christmas tree lights, or on the main fuse box. When he was electrocuted, the lights fused. At the time, Diana and I thought it was a glitch in the mains supply, but we know better now. Jane would have had to rewire the plug and the socket to cover her tracks. And she must have gone down to the cellar to repair the fuse or turn the circuit breaker back on. She wouldn't have had occasion to touch those in the usual run of things. I doubt she'd even have good reason to know where the fuse box is. Try it," I urged.

And that's how Evie came to be charged with the murder of her son. If I'd thought things through, if I'd waited till my brain was out of shock, I'd have realized that Jane would never have risked her baby by hauling Edmund's body over the crossbar of his mountain bike and wheeling him out to the copse. Besides, she probably believed she could use his love for her to persuade him to change his mind. Evie didn't have that hope to cling to.

If I'd realized it was Diana's mother who killed Edmund, I doubt very much if I'd have shared my esoteric knowledge with DI Staniforth. It's a funny business, New Age medicine. When I attended a seminar on the healing powers of plants given by a Native American medicine man, I never thought his wisdom would help me prove a murder.

Maybe Evie will get lucky. Maybe she'll get a jury reluctant to convict in a case that rests on the inexplicable fact that lightning never strikes birch trees.

# Author Biographies

**Kris Brandenburger** is a writer and poet whose work has appeared in *Zyzzyva*, *Violet Ink*, *The L.A. Review*, and more. Until recently, her work has been repairing the electrical systems of exotic automobiles. She is now academic director of the undergraduate degree completion program at New College of California in San Francisco.

**Holly Farris** is an Appalachian who has worked as an autopsy assistant, restaurant baker, and beekeeper. She has been nominated twice for the Pushcart Prize. *Lockjaw*, Holly's first collection of literary short fiction, will be published by Gival Press in 2007.

**Katherine V. Forrest** is the internationally known author of 15 works of fiction, including the lesbian classic, *Curious Wine*, the lesbian-feminist utopian trilogy that began with *Daughters of the Coral Dawn*, and the Kate Delafield mystery series which is a three-time winner of the Lambda Literary Award. She has edited numerous anthologies, and her stories, articles and reviews have appeared in publications worldwide. She was senior editor at Naiad Press for ten years, and continues to edit as well as teach classes in the craft of fiction. She lives with her partner in San Francisco.

**R. Gay** is a writer and graduate student whose writing can be found in many anthologies, including *Best American Erotica 2004*, several editions of *Best Lesbian Erotica*, *Far From Home: Father Daughter Travel Adventures* and others.

**Barbara Kahn** is a playwright, director, and actor. Her plays have been produced in Los Angeles, San Diego, Boston, Philadelphia, and New York. Theater for the New City, now in its 31st year, has been the New York City home for Barbara's plays since 1994, including *War Bonds* in May 2002. Barbara received the 1995 Torch of Hope Award for lifetime achievement, whose past recipients include Terrence McNally, August Wilson and Horton Foote. She has twice received production grants from the Arch and Bruce Brown Foundation, in support of gay-positive theatre based on history. Barbara's work was most recently published in *Even More Monologues for Women by Women* (Heinemann) and *Harrington Lesbian Fiction Quarterly* (Haworth Press). She is a member of the Dramatics Guild and a founding member of Sisters On Stage. Visit her website at www.barbara-kahn.com.

**Lee Lynch** has been writing lesbian fiction stories and articles since the 1960's. Her new novel, *Sweet Creek*, has been published by Bold Strokes Books. Her column, "The Amazon Trail," is celebrating its 20th anniversary and is syndicated in lesbian, gay and PFLAG publications nationwide. She lives in the Pacific Northwest.

**Val McDermid** grew up in a Scottish mining community and then read English at Oxford. She was a journalist for sixteen years before devoting herself full-time to writing. She is an international best-seller and her psychological thriller *The Mermaids Singing* won the 1995 Gold Dagger Award for Best Crime Novel of the Year. She lives in the North of England. Visit her website at www.valmcdermid.com.

**Kathy Porter** is a writer who lives near the U.S.-Mexico border.

**Cynthia J. Price** has spent half a lifetime living with her wife on the coast of Kwa Zulu Natal, South Africa, where they have raised two children, one poodle, and numerous cats. As a remnant from the 60's, she is a rare combination of serious banker during working hours and a bare-footed, back-packing hippy during loafing hours. This is her 4th short story to be published and she is threatening to continue writing until her sanity improves.

**Jane Rule** was born in New Jersey in 1931 and graduated from Mills College in California. She moved to Canada in 1956, where she taught at the University of British Columbia until 1976 when she moved to Galiano Island. In 1978 she won the Canadian Authors Association Best Novel of the Year Award for *The Young in One Another's Arms*. The film *Desert Hearts* is based on her novel, *Desert of the Heart*.

**Rita Stumps** lives in California's San Fernando Valley with her life partner, Judy, and cat, Desi. Previous publications have appeared in *LSF: Lesbian Short Fiction*,

*Women Runners: Stories of Transformation*, and *How Running Changed My Life*. Rita and Judy celebrate every holiday imaginable, and are especially busy in December, when Christmas, Hanukkah, and their two birthdays usually fall within a two-week period.

**Valarie Watersun** became a published author at eleven with a poem in a children's magazine. This acceptance led to a lifetime devoted to the written word. In subsequent years her stories and poems appeared in dozens of magazines across the U.S. from *Ellipsis* (west coast) to *Lynchburg Magazine* (east coast). During a ten-year career as a reporter, her feature stories appeared in periodicals such as *Virginia Review* and *Scene* magazine. In 2004, Watersun's first commercial novel, *The Quality of Blue*, was released. Her book review column appears in quarterly issues of *The Wishing Well* magazine. Visit her website at www.valariewatersun.com.

**Zonna** was a prolific songwriter and author, and a seven-time *Billboard Magazine* songwriting contest winner. She wrote stories for anthologies by Alyson Publications, Arsenal Pulp Press, Black Books, and Seal Press and released over a half-dozen recordings, including her acclaimed 1997 album "Carved In Stone." She died on December 1st, 2003, from complications due to diabetes and colon cancer, at age 43.

# PERMISSIONS

"Dallying with Llamas," by Kris Brandenburger. Copyright © 2006 by Kris Brandenburger.

"Tiny Dancer," by Holly Farris. Copyright © 2000 by Holly Farris.

"The Gift," by Katherine V. Forrest. Copyright © 1987 by Katherine V. Forrest. First published in *Dreams and Swords* by Katherine V. Forrest, Naiad Press. Reprinted by permission of the author.

"All in the Seasoning," by R. Gay. Copyright © 1999 by R. Gay.

"Winter Solstice: The Cat's Meow," by Barbara Kahn. Copyright © 1998 by Barbara Kahn.

"Hanukkah in a Bar," by Lee Lynch. Copyright © 1994 by Lee Lynch. First published in *Cactus Love* by Lee Lynch, Naiad Press. Reprinted by permission of the author.

"Fires of Winter Solstice," by Lee Lynch. Copyright © 1994 by Lee Lynch. First published in *Cactus Love* by Lee Lynch, Naiad Press. Reprinted by permission of the author.

"A Traditional Christmas," by V. L. McDermid. Copyright © 1994 by V. L. McDermid. First published in *Reader, I*

# Bywater Books

## DANCE IN THE KEY OF LOVE

### Marianne K. Martin

"Marianne Martin is a wonderful storyteller and a graceful writer with a light, witty touch ..."
—Ann Bannon, author of the Beebo Brinker series

Paige Flemming is on the run. From the police, from her history, and from love itself. After sixteen years looking over her shoulder, she realizes it's time to run again. But when she pauses in her headlong flight to catch her breath with old friends, she crashes straight into another ghost from her past. And this time, it's not one she can easily escape.

In this long-awaited sequel to the best-selling lesbian romance *Dawn of the Dance*, Lambda Literary Award finalist Marianne K. Martin reminds us that there's no footwork fancy enough to dance out of the shadow of the past.

Paperback Original • ISBN 1-932859-17-9 • $13.95

Available at your local bookstore
or call toll-free 866-390-7426
or order online at www.bywaterbooks.com